Jack Commer, Supreme Commander

Book Two of the Jack Commer Series

Michael D. Smith

Sortmind Press, 2020
press.sortmind.com

For my wife Nancy

CHAPTER ONE
Jack's Anxiety
Thursday, February 1, 2035, 2336 hours

Jack studied his console and nodded wearily at Joe to his right. "Check."

"Check," his brother muttered from the copilot seat, the window by his head blazing with jagged, multicolored streaks of light. "Drive pressure indicator?"

"Check."

"Check. Okay, that's it for *this* list." Joe clicked his USSF Comm and squinted at the next page, face slack and ashen, mirroring Jack's own exhaustion. "Great, we don't have to do this next page until the Eight-Minute Check."

"Good, we're done with Six. We can use the break." Jack spoke into the intercom: "Connors, we'll be out of Star Drive in eight minutes forty seconds. Be ready to pick up our position."

"Roger," came Will Connors' reply over the intercom. "NAV4 Cluster's set to go the instant we're out of Drive. All preliminary programs--check."

"Check ..." Jack sighed.

"Check," Joe said automatically.

"Damn." Jack punched the intercom again. "All stations, status check."

"Jack, they just reported *in* a half minute ago."

"I just want to make sure." Jack scanned his own comm. "We need to be ready when Eight comes up."

"No, I think you're just too burned out to know what you're doing anymore, and you can't keep still." Joe lay down his comm and closed his eyes. "Me, I'm gonna sit back and enjoy my minute-and-a-half break."

"Radio and radar all clear, everything okay!" Patrick James screeched over the intercom.

"Check ..." Jack muttered. He shut his eyes as well. He considered turning down the harsh white glare of the Control Room lights, but he knew the chaotic stream of starlight outside, jerking in thousands of colors, would make his headache worse.

1

He drifted, and was awakened by:

"Navigation! This is Connors! Everything ready like I just said a second ago!"

"Borman here. Dorsal turret *perfect*."

"Idiot," Jack snorted. They'd all been on board *Typhoon II* for almost twenty hours, and every time Jack had spoken to Borman, the gunner said every instrument in his turret was "perfect." People who thought that everything was perfect were asking for trouble.

"Ventral turret ... office of the physician/engineer ... and chief librarian ... all check out," came Phil Sperry's drawl from the rear of the ship. Jack could picture Sperry upside down in his turret, in his reverse gravity field, a few feet from the Star Drive reactor. "Yep, it's all *perfect,* Admiral."

Jack grinned. "Check." To his right, his brother appeared to be asleep.

"Pod," came the deep female voice from the intercom. "Everything checks out here, Jack. The Martians have calmed down, but not as much as I'd hoped. I thought the freak-out would pass once they'd had a few minutes of the Drive, but Dar says it's wrecking their Thought Fields."

"Well, nothing we can do about it now. Tell 'em to hold on." Jack regretted overriding Amav's suggestion that each Martian be strapped down in his own quarters. Instead he'd listened to Dar, who'd thought it best if the Martians could sit quietly and meditate in the central recreation room of the saucer-shaped Pod slung beneath the *Typhoon*. All had gone well until the first seconds of Star Drive, when the Martians had begun shrieking, ripping up pillows, and lunging for each other and Amav. She'd exhausted forty tranquilizer darts before Dar, Kner, and Fulr had shown the least sign of settling down. For the last five minutes she'd been alternately counseling them, babying them, and firing drugs into their chests.

Jack shifted uneasily and checked his watch. Thirty seconds to go before the Eight-Minute Check. He didn't like the idea of a Pod attached to his sleek ship in the first place. It was like carting around a fashionable Marsport condominium, with its huge central recreation room, sixteen personal compartments for use by the three Martians and seven humans on the flight, as well as negotiation rooms where, everyone hoped, treaties would be hammered out with the Alpha Centaurians. The saucer had a kitchen, food to last a year, showers, and exercise machines. It also had sixty-four Xon bombs in the lower compartment. These, added to the normal complement of four Xons in the *Typhoon II's* nose, along with the powerful pair of PlanetBlasters mounted on the back and belly of the craft, gave Jack the capability of destroying several solar systems in the course of an eight-hour work day. If negotiations failed.

"Jack!" Amav cried. "I'm running out of darts! Do you think you could spare one of the turret men to come help me with the Martians?"

"Negative! Listen, Amav, I'm sorry if it's hard down there, but we're busy up here ourselves."

"I'll be right over," Sperry called in. His red light came on the Crew Locator Console, indicating movement from his last assigned position. Jack traced the orange dots moving down to the Pod.

"*Dammit,* Phil," Jack hissed. With his old-fashioned chivalrousness, Phil had been easy prey for Amav's silly pleadings throughout this project. She needed help with this, she needed help with that. Jack had been trying to wean her away from dependence on the other crewmembers, but Phil kept offering to do her duties. Why was she making such a fuss over three hyper Martians?

"Hey, Jack, it's okay," Phil spoke over the intercom. "I'll just be gone a second. We can't do anything in the turrets during Star Drive anyway. And we can't let those Martians run amok."

"Yeah, right," Jack snarled. Sperry had been dropping hints for the last few weeks about how hard Jack had been pushing Amav. Now he was implying Jack wasn't concerned for her safety.

"I swear, Dar, I don't want to shoot any more darts at you!" came the cry from below. "But if I have to, I will!"

"You would shoot darts at *me?* The Emperor of the

Martians?" came the hysterical shriek.

"Just sit down, Dar, and behave!"

"No! I won't! I won't! I absolutely *refuse!*"

Ka-chuk! Ka-chuk! Ka-chuk!

"Jack, I've got Dar on the floor now, but I'm out of darts! And Kner's starting to froth at the mouth again!"

"C'mon, Amav, cut the dramatics!" Jack shouted. "Just lock 'em in there and get the hell out!"

"Amav!" Sperry cried. "What's going on?"

"I need darts! Thousands of them! These Martians are going berserk!"

"There's a roll of 'em in the auxiliary medical locker," Sperry said. "Some force field handcuffs'll come in handy as well."

"Oh, thanks, Phil, we just need to hold them a while longer. I'm afraid they'll claw each other to death if we leave them alone!"

"Dammit, dammit, *dammit!*" Jack slapped at the intercom buttons. "All this useless chatter! Wake up, Joe, for God's sake, we've missed the Eight-Minute Check!"

"Hey, Jack, cool it. I've been awake all this time. I'm starting on Eight right now."

Jack snatched up Joe's comm. "Aw, come on, let's cut the crap! Any fool can see everything's okay. I'll be damned if I'll sit here for five minutes checking off these goddamn instruments all over again. Let's just forget this mindless junk!" He mashed the delete button for the checklist and tossed the comm back at Joe. "Okay?"

"Whew."

"Don't act so damn superior."

"Jack, I know we're all tired. But just remember that's all it is. So we've all been up for twenty hours. So what?"

"It was just such poor timing to launch at 2300, and only get into Star Drive just now!"

"Well, you're head of the USSF, brother. Why didn't you change the time?"

"Hell, those damn technicians *forced* me into it."

"C'mon, Jack."

"And if we hadn't had to do that damn interview at 1900!"

Joe shrugged. "Good publicity, I guess. We were already running so far behind that another hour didn't really hurt."

"The hell with it. Forget the whole stupid thing. I hate Star Drive, Joe, I just hate it! I mean, look at all that crap!" He indicated the jagged streaks of light flashing past.

"Look, I know what you mean. I'd rather be seeing normal stars myself. But it's your first Star Drive, after all. Give it time."

"It's your first Star Drive too!" Jack shot back. "And you say *you're* enjoying it?"

Joe shifted in his seat. "Well, I suppose it affects us a little bit like the Martians, but that's no reason to hate the concept of Star Drive. I mean, it's opened up the galaxy to us, after all."

"It's opened up the stinking Alpha Centaurian war, you mean. That's all it's been good for! I'm sick of it! Star Drive is *junk!* Who needs it? We're not ready for the whole galaxy is what I think!"

"Jack, what in the world is the matter with you?"

Jack shook his head. "Hey, Joe, I'm sorry. I really don't know."

"It's the Star Drive. We're all affected by it. You just need to take it easy. You've been worrying yourself sick about this mission for months."

"Well … maybe."

"And you're probably just a little out of shape for this flight. We all are. We haven't had a real flight in six months. No wonder we're out of shape."

"Yeah, maybe that's a part of it." Shuttling the *Typhoon II* between Earth and Mars, and assisting the Martians with their Amplified Thought program for restoring the earth, certainly didn't count as real spaceflight. In a way Jack had never recovered from the Hergs war eight months ago. Never allowed himself to. The entire crew of *Typhoon I* lost. Their two younger brothers dead.

And all along he'd been thinking he'd been on top of it all.

"Yeah …" he repeated. "All the stuff that's been going on.

Like this USSF thing. Maybe that's been the main thing."

"The whole Supreme Commander business?"

Jack nodded. His promotion to Supreme Commander of the United System Space Force four weeks ago had been dismaying, not only to Jack, but to the entire *Typhoon* crew and thousands of officers who'd been passed over. The only way Jack could deal with it was to joke about being "Admiral Commer" and about how much power he had. His decision to remain in command of the *Typhoon II* and manage the entire USSF bureaucracy via superspace radio during this negotiation mission in Alpha Centauri had further strained his sanity. Jack now held full authority to launch military operations in the name of the United System anywhere in this part of the galaxy, now that Star Drive could theoretically take them to hundreds of neighboring stars. Sure, there was the United System Council that nominally controlled the USSF, but in practice the Council left all military decisions up to the SCUSSF, the Supreme Commander of the USSF. Jack Commer had just become the most powerful human being who'd ever lived.

"Yeah," Jack sighed. "It's all this USSF stuff. You should see how much paperwork I've got in my locker. I can't believe Scott handed me three dozen notebooks filled with *paper*."

"Well, he really never used his comm for anything but a glorified telephone," Joe grinned. "Yeah, I saw you loading all that crap of his in there."

"And this Star Drive business just seems like more bureaucracy, Joe. You don't feel the ship, for God's sake! You just see these idiotic *lights*."

"Those are *stars* being distorted by the effects of the Drive."

"I know what they are! They're *junk*. There's no piloting, Joe. Just tell Connors to plot a course, and bam, fifteen minutes later we're in Alpha Centauri."

"Well, there'll be time for piloting when we come out of the Drive."

"But that's also what I'm afraid of. We come out of Drive, and what are we? That's right, we're sitting ducks, going the same speed when we engaged the drive, 4,000 miles per hour.

That's *pitiful*. A whole fleet of Centaurians could be on top of us before we get up to speed. If we could do the Drive at one-fifth light, that'd be one thing. But we're really running a risk here, and I don't like it."

Joe turned to his comm. "Coming up on the Ten-Minute Check."

"Forget it. Let's just blow that off, okay? We can see full well we don't need a check."

"Jack, the rules--"

"Forget the rules! I *am* the rules! We've run that check a thousand times today, and it's silly to just do it over and over when we can see exactly what's going on in this ship from the command console." He waved at his instruments. "Everything's okay!"

"Everything's *perfect,*" Joe mocked.

Jack grimaced. "Okay, okay, I get the point, run the damn list."

"No, I agree it's stupid. But let's do Fourteen just to make sure, okay?"

"All right. We'll do a Fourteen. I just need to get away from this sense of *bureaucracy* for a while."

"And I guess it doesn't help anything to have your wife along on the trip."

Jack straightened up. "No, that has nothing to do with how I'm feeling."

"C'mon, Jack, you've been all over poor Amav ever since we got on board today. You've been at her for weeks now. Everyone's noticed it."

"Joe, that's none of your business. Everything between Amav and me is fine. Just fine."

"Just *perfect,*" Joe repeated. But his brown eyes were filled with concern.

Jack expelled some air. "Yeah, just perfect. I guess. I don't suppose you'd want your latest girlfriend on board. What's her name? Laurel?"

Joe's face darkened. Jack knew Joe only got to see his current flame every three or four weeks on the New Luna run.

Laurel was a colonist on Earth's new artificial moon, and Jack had never seen Joe as wrapped up in a woman before. Finally Joe said: "Laurel's wonderful. But I don't think I'd want her on board the *Typhoon*. We'd just drive each other crazy. I wouldn't want to mix work and pleasure like that."

Jack looked at the floor. When he and Amav had married in July, this whole mission had seemed like a metaphor for an open, powerful relationship that Jack would never have believed possible. And now? "Well, you know, I never told anyone this, because I knew if Scott had found out, he might've blocked my promotion. He would've *crucified* me if he'd found out that the real reason I kept delaying this mission was so Amav could finish up her Ph.D. in December."

"You mean," Joe said, "that's the reason for all those delays about the design of the Pod, and how it'd interface with the *Typhoon,* and all those programming updates?"

"C'mon, you know all that was worked out by September. It was just a few simple modifications to an existing design. We could've launched mid-October with no sweat. But Amav couldn't have come. Or she could've, I guess, but God knows when she would've finished her degree." His motives for letting Amav finish her Ph.D. hadn't been entirely selfish. A listing on his ship's roster of "Dr. Amav Frankston-Commer, Planetary Engineer," might look good to the Alpha Centaurians, who'd seen scores of their agricultural worlds laid waste by USSF starships and might clutch at expert help in repairing them.

Joe leaned back and scrutinized his brother. "Jack, that is *awful.* That's like a *sin* against the USSF. You should be ashamed of yourself."

"Really?" Jack blurted. "You really think so? But I didn't mean any harm, really! I mean, really, if you'd only *understand,* Joe."

"I do understand. I understand that you've jeopardized the most important negotiation mission in the history of humanity just so wifey could tag along."

"I ... I ..." Jack looked away. Tears welled up. "God, you're right. Why don't you place me under arrest, then?"

But Joe was cackling in his chair, swiveling wildly. "God! You really fell for it! You really fell for it!"

"Fell … for what?"

"Fell for it! Hell, Jack, do I care why you held up the flight? Does anybody? Did Scott even? Hell, no! We all knew it would be convenient if the flight was held up till Amav got done. We even thought it would be best if you held it up until after Scott named you SCUSSF. So did Scott, if you really want to know. He told me that if you couldn't start by August, then you should probably wait until you became USSF head in January."

"God, you really think no one cares?"

"Of course no one cares! Jack, you're Supreme Commander! It's entirely up to you when any spaceship in the fleet is launched. Especially your own flagship! The technicians who programmed the 2300 launch would've easily postponed it a few hours to let us get some sleep! If you'd just *ordered* them to!"

"Really? You think? Well, of course they would! You know, Joe, we've been on the *Typhoon* project for what? Seven years now? And I never flinched once from command. Well, between you and me, once or twice, but I can't understand why this USSF thing is *throwing* me so much."

"You're just not used to it all yet. Give it time, and you'll be the best USSF head there ever will be. I know it."

"Well, thanks."

"And look, Jack, it's not just the USSF thing. Everyone can see it. It's Amav. Everyone can tell. The two of you don't belong on the same ship, and you know it."

"Okay, okay. I guess you're right. That damned Pod! She *insisted* we have that Pod attached to the ship! It's so ugly!"

"She was responsible for that? I thought the Council Negotiation Committee wanted the Pod."

"Hell, no, she knew the Martians would need a lot of space if we dragged 'em along. And she knew she'd need quarters if we dragged *her* along. And she kept saying we had to have a regular place for negotiations with the Centaurians. Well, she was right, I guess, at least about those Martians. I mean, they're *wimps,* you know?"

"Jack, really," Joe said in mock consternation.

"Hell, you know it's true." Of course, they all loved their Martian friends. It was just that the Martians were so hypersensitive that it was often impossible to speak a single sentence without somehow offending them. And the rigors of space travel, and especially Star Drive, were tearing up the Martians' fragile central nervous systems.

"And Amav," Jack went on, "I mean, she's *everywhere.* I never escape her. And look at what's coming up. Sure, it's just a fifteen-minute journey to Alpha Centauri, but it could be *months* of negotiations with the Centaurians. We'll all be on this ship for *months.* I'm exhausted as it is."

"It's been a strain for you, I know. I can see you need a vacation. You've been supervising this project and getting the whole USSF bureaucracy in your lap the last few weeks. And I know Amav was on overdrive to finish her degree up the past few months."

"Vacations," Jack spat. "They just delude you."

"Are you kidding? You told me you had the time of your life in July!"

Jack shrugged. That conversation with Joe back in August had been their last serious talk. For six months the brothers had been bantering and superficial. "Well, I meant it then. We spent that whole month in Alaska making plans for solving the whole war in Alpha Centauri in one stroke. But somehow we were totally relaxed the whole time. And I thought, this vacation is a vision of what life could be like. And then, when we got back to work ..." Jack couldn't bring himself to discuss the mindless arguments, the way Amav manipulated Jack to get her way, the compromises she made to his command. This whole mission definitely had Amav's stamp on it. *She'd* designed the whole damn thing. *She* was running the show. Jack Commer, Supreme Commander--what a farce.

Jack checked his console. "Dammit, Sperry's still not back to his turret! And now *Borman's* out of place! Where's he going? Can't we maintain *any* discipline here?"

CHAPTER TWO
Borman

There was a knock on the Control Room hatch, which swung open before Jack or Joe could respond. Lee Borman stood there, a chunky, crew-cut little guy with a toothy smile. "Hello, gents. What happened to the Eight-Minute Check? Or the Ten-Minute Check for that matter," he added, glancing at his watch.

"All right, back to your station, Lee," Jack snapped. "We're blowing off checks until Fourteen."

Borman lounged in the entrance, one hand to the top of the hatch. "Hey, Admiral, that's against the regs."

"Lieutenant, to your turret immediately!"

"Hey, wow, Jack, I mean, *Monsieur Admiral,*" Borman said, rolling his eyes.

"He doesn't mean it," Joe offered. "He's tired. We all are."

"But *I* mean it!" Jack shouted, coming out of his chair. "Borman, you pinhead, outa here! Right now! Or so help me God!"

"Whoa, man, remember me, baby? Lee Borman, man, I mean, *Admiral.*"

"And you can cut the damn Admiral jokes!"

"Hey, Admiral, like I'm real serious, man," Borman smirked.

By this time Joe was also on his feet. "What's gotten into you, Lee? Get back to your post. Are you crazy?"

"I'm not leaving." Borman folded his arms and braced himself firmly in the hatchway. "Admiral Commer's gone nuts, I see." He flashed Jack a mindless grin. "Buddy, you really *have* been a pain recently."

"Outa my control room! Right now!"

"See, the guy's snapped," Borman said to Joe. "It's my thinking that he needs a little talking to, and he'll be perfectly fine."

"Lieutenant, are you drunk?" Joe said. "Have you been drinking?"

"Why, hell, no, Commander Commer," Borman grinned.

11

"Why do you say that?"

"Because, Lieutenant Borman, you smell of booze, that's why! Jack, I recommend we confine him to the Pod. We can't have this!"

Jack had been staring into Borman's bloodshot eyes for several giddy seconds, and his mind was a whirlpool. He couldn't believe the first-name, close-friends basis of the *Typhoon II* had unraveled like this. Then again, Borman had started it. All this stuff about his turret being perfect, his increasing insolence, and his constant denigrating of Jack's new command. "Borman, go … go home," Jack said, waving loosely at the back of the ship. He could see down the fifty-foot, brightly-lighted cylinder with the escape craft parked on the floor. The small compartments for sensor, navigation, dorsal weapon turret and other instrumentation ranged down the upper starboard quarter of the cylinder, and Jack saw Patrick James' and Will Connors' legs outside their doors. Abruptly Jack jerked Borman inside and slammed the Control Room hatch. It wouldn't do to have the rest listening to this.

Borman stumbled forward, caught off guard, and sprawled beside Joe's chair.

"Drunk," Jack said in disgust. He'd expected Borman to simply pass out, and so was surprised when Borman staggered to his feet and swung a vicious punch. It came nowhere close, and now Joe had Borman in a hammerlock.

"All right, all right, lemme go. I was just kiddin'," Borman sneered.

"Lee, what the hell has gotten into you?" Jack burst out. "I can't believe this!"

"Borman, you're under arrest," Joe said, struggling to keep Borman in place. But Borman wasn't seriously resisting.

"Belay that. Borman, you are *not* under arrest. Joe, let him go."

"But, Jack--"

"Forget it. We can't waste time on this. All right, Lee, I want a simple explanation of your behavior and I want it right now. I'm sorry if I was irritable and I'm sorry if it set you off. But you do realize that as captain of this ship I have the right to be irritable with anyone on board."

"Except wifey, I presume," Borman said, getting to his feet and making exaggerated motions of dusting himself off.

"What's *that* supposed to mean?"

"C'mon, Jack, everyone knows you're uptight about Amav being on board. The whole ship's suffering as a result. It's *hell* working with you, man. And ever since you became Monsieur Hotshot Admiral SCUSSF, you've been *really* intolerable."

"Jack, we just cannot have this! On board the *Typhoon,* in wartime!" Joe cried, hand on his shattergun. Jack waved him away. God, that it had come to this flare-up, over nothing. This was the most ill-conceived mission Jack had ever done. But he forced himself to go through the motions of acting like a ship's captain. Somebody had to clean this mess up. Might as well be Jack.

"Borman, I'm going to overlook this transgression this time," Jack said. "In the future, I will expect you to treat myself, my position, and everyone on board this ship with the dignity that our mission requires."

"Aw, forget it, dude!" Borman hooted. "We all just wanna go back to the nice, informal way we had it before. Before all this *crap* started."

"That will not be possible, Lieutenant," Jack said coldly. "We are in a new era."

"We are in a new era," Borman said in a singsong.

Jack exhaled. Joe had abandoned the discussion to check his console. It reminded Jack that this little flap had best be gotten over with in a hurry.

And yet the sight of Borman, swaying back and forth, obviously plastered, made Jack want to delve right into the complicated mess at full throttle. "I assume, Lieutenant, that your little revolt here has something to do with my refusal to allow the turrets full freedom of shooting?"

"Aw, Jack, you are such a tight little twit."

Joe twisted around and glared. But he wasn't about to speak for Jack again.

Jack sighed. Borman, who'd been a sensational turret gunner in Alpha Centauri, had been itching for PlanetBlaster action for months. During his four-month stint in 2033, Borman had shot down a record 4,068 enemy spacecraft and had made the cover of *Mars Magazine*. On the little three-man fighters, neither the pilot nor the navigator had any say about when and what to fire at. The turret man in effect commanded the ship, using his medium-barrel PlanetBlaster to burn whatever he felt necessary. So it grated on Borman when Jack had ordered that the *Typhoon's* oversized PlanetBlasters, the most powerful lasers humanity had developed, be kept strictly under Jack's control. Not only had this been Jack's rule aboard the *Typhoon I,* but the *Typhoon II* was now officially engaged on a peace mission. Sperry, the other turret man, hadn't cared. He'd done a three-month training hitch in AC a year ago, and though he'd destroyed 555 enemy craft, he never developed Borman's bloodlust. And here was Borman itching to burn entire enemy fleets with one sizzle of his giant dorsal turret gun, or evaporate planetary oceans in seconds and watch the crust beneath melt like a giant pizza.

"I don't care about your damn order," Borman said. "I know if I see an AC I'll probably just whip the gun around in total reflex action, man. Vaporize the wimps. That's how I survived before. I didn't wait for some pansy pilot to make my decisions for me."

"Lieutenant Borman, if I seriously thought you were to disobey my PlanetBlaster order I would not hesitate to use my shattergun on you this second." He probed for fear in Borman's eyes, got the barest flicker. If only Borman, or any of the *Typhoon II* crew, knew of yet another innovation the *Typhoon II* possessed over the destroyed *Typhoon I:* the anti-personnel lasers mounted in all compartments, in the turrets, even in the Control Room. A touch of Jack's USSF Comm could fry Will Connors right now if he so desired. Or Borman here, though Jack would have to hit the floor quickly to avoid being charred himself. The paranoid designers of the *Typhoon II* had worried about mutiny. Well, Jack thought grimly, maybe they were right.

God, could it really be that the Star Drive was doing this to them? Changing them into surly animals?

"Commer," Borman growled. "You must think you're a real he-man. You think because you've got such a hot broad that you're a real stud."

"Jack, I really recommend we lock this guy up right now," Joe said, turning. "We're about a minute from Fourteen now, and we can't afford this."

"Shut up, wimp. This is between Jocko and me."

"After this mission, Borman, you and me--neural stunners, plutonium knives, shatterguns, you name it. I'll take you on anywhere, anytime," Joe said beneath his breath, turning back to his work.

"Jerk," Borman muttered. "I just want you idiots to know that I came up here because, see, I know how to help Jack with his masculine inferiority complexes. I could cure him, and fast, and we wouldn't have to worry about this Amav chick screwing up the mission."

"Borman, that is my *wife* you're referring to!" Jack snarled.

"C'mon, Jack, everyone knows how badly she's blown this mission. And how you can't take it."

"How? How in blazes does everyone know that?"

"You jerk! Everyone can hear it!" Borman pointed to Jack's command station. Jack stared in dismay. The intercom to the rest of the ship was on. Everyone had heard everything. He ran to the switch. At least the Pod intercom had been switched off, but the rest of the crew in the *Typhoon* proper had heard his whole conversation with Joe. Amav. Deceiving Scott. The Ph.D. Everything. He whirled to the plastered turret gunner. "Borman, you are hereby under arrest!" To his consternation Jack found his shattergun in hand, drawing a bead on Borman's thick ugly red nose. This time Borman raised his eyebrows.

"Say, Jack," Joe said. "I'm getting a low reading on Power Thruster Six. It's not too bad, but the heat--"

"Forget it!" Jack said. "This guy's under arrest! I won't have him insulting Amav like that!"

"But can't you see, Jack, that's your whole *problem,* man,"

Borman began babbling, eyes locked onto the shattergun. "You've always been so *repressed* around women that you've let this Amav take over your sense of *self-esteem.* If you'd only *actualize* your *potential,* Jack, and learn to recognize those parts of yourself which--"

"So you've sobered up pretty fast, Lieutenant," Jack mocked. "Back to your self-help clichés, I see." Unbelievably, Borman had recently gotten a publisher's contract for a self-help book for men called *The Sexual Conquest of Your Inner Mount Everest.* To the entire crew's chagrin, he'd printed paper copies for everyone. Jack had read part of one chapter entitled "Finding your F-Spot" and had thrown the thick manuscript away.

That a chunky fighter veteran of the Alpha Centauri conflict was writing self-help books on the subject of male sexuality was beyond the comprehension of any of the crew, and it had only come out haltingly, over a period of months, that the other five members of *Typhoon II* admitted that they'd thrown their manuscripts away unread. But Borman had become more and more egotistical about his book as the mission got closer to launch date. He'd even given copies to Amav and the three Martians. Amav never said a word. Dar had briefly commented: "You humans are one million years behind us."

"Okay, Jack, just--okay," Borman swallowed. "We all have our hang-ups. I know I did, once. But I *learned,* Jack. I went *inside* myself, I took the *dare,* and I climbed my *own* Mount Everest! I'm here today to tell you that if you'd only climb *yours*--"

"Getting sorta nervous, Lee baby?" Jack sneered. "You're kinda thinking that old Jack boy's just crazy enough to turn you into a pile of broken glass? Huh? Huh? Well, Lee baby, maybe I am that crazy. Maybe I am." It was so exciting to hold a gun on the criminal Borman. To feel his finger caressing the trigger with mounting pressure. For once everyone would know exactly how Jack could express himself. Fully and finally express himself. God, it felt so good, such a sweet release of all the hate and tension and anger and fear--

"Jack! You can't!" Borman cried, looking down the barrel

of the shattergun. "Jack! For God's sake! We're *friends,* old buddy!"

At last Jack had the look in Borman's eyes that he wanted. "I'd like to remind you of one thing, Lee baby. I know you climbed Everest back in '25, way before the Final War. But you stand there, thinking I won't pull this trigger and rid my ship of a traitor during wartime, and you forget ... how that war ended."

"Jack, that Thruster Six pressure drop doesn't look so good. And where the hell's Sperry?" Joe said. "Sperry! Get out of the Pod! Thruster Six is critical!"

"Joe! Buddy! This guy's insane!" Borman moaned. "Help me!"

"We're past Fourteen. Pressure on Six down to 12.3."

"Joe!" Borman screamed.

"You forget how the Final War ended! Don't you?" Jack hissed.

"No! No! I didn't forget! I do know! I admit I'm drunk! Yeah, I got drunk! I couldn't handle the Star Drive, Jack! I couldn't! I'm sorry!"

"You forgot how the war ended when you wrote the stupid title of your stupid book! Didn't you, traitor? Answer me-- traitor!"

"I--I was trying to answer the *absence* of ... oh God!"

"*I* dropped the Xon bomb on the Central Asians! *I* dug the damn crater a hundred miles deep! There's no Mount Everest anymore, Lee baby! No Himalayas, no India, no Persia, not much of China! It's all gone, baby! And why? Why? I'll tell you why! Because Jack Commer was crazy enough to go through with it! It was the only way, Lee baby. Scott gave me the order, and I swallowed long and hard, but we had to do it. Had to drop the Xon. Had to do it, Lee baby, you hear me?"

"Yeah, God, yeah ... Jack, *please!*"

"And so you do realize, Lee baby, that I'm crazy enough to follow through on my threats?"

"Jack--*please!*"

"I'm crazy enough to blow Everest to blazes! I'm crazy enough to shatter you all over the floor! I've never liked you,

Borman! Never!"

The Control Room hatch snapped open. Sperry stood there, six-five, his dark hair flying in all directions, his deep-set eyes wild.

"Sperry! Number Six!" Joe grunted.

"Get back! Get back!" Jack screamed, waving his shattergun.

"He's gonna execute me!" Borman whimpered.

"I know! I heard it all back in the ship!" Sperry cried. "Jack, just get back!"

"You can't order me around, mister!" Jack shouted.

"Pressure 6.9 and dropping!" Joe called.

"Are we gonna black-hole? Are we gonna black-hole?" came a shout from down the fuselage.

"Jack! Get a hold of yourself! It's Star Drive!" Sperry shouted. "It's just tension and moodiness! Let's laugh it off, Jack! For God's sake, Joe, hit the thruster *reverse feed!*"

"Dammit, Phil, why aren't you down at your post?" Joe yelled back. "We're twenty seconds from coming out of Star Drive and Number Six is *toast!*"

"Amav had trouble with the damned Martians! I had to deal with them!"

"That's insane, Sperry! Insane! Dereliction of duty! Dereliction of duty!" Jack screamed. "You're under arrest! You and everybody else aboard this ship! I won't have you knowing *anything* about Amav!"

He raised his shattergun at Sperry. But from the corner of his eye Jack saw a metal plate bursting loose from an assembly at the rear of the ship. It tumbled end over end down the fuselage toward them. A muffled explosion followed.

CHAPTER THREE
Star Drive at 14:46

Despite the shock of Jack waving the shattergun in his face, Phil knew instantly what had happened.

The stars were pinpoints of light again. "The Drive! Joe, what's the pressure?"

"Zero. All thrusters out," Joe replied. "Number Six took down the other nine."

"My God! Sperry! Are we leaking air?" Jack cried, pointing to a cloud of gray gas in the fuselage.

"Jack, put that thing away!" Phil shouted, pointing to Jack's gun.

"No! *Borman's* here! My God! The air!"

"It's just gas to put out any fires! If we were leaking air, we'd have lost all of it by now!"

Jack straightened and holstered his shattergun. He looked out the windows. "So we're out of Drive," he said in disgust.

"Moving 4,000 miles per hour," Joe said. "Same as we started."

"Out of Star Drive," came Connors' call from the Navigation Room. "I'm plotting our location now."

"Dammit!" Jack spat. "Sperry, why the hell did your damn engine have to screw up like this?"

Phil turned and made his way down the corridor to the engine. He'd had enough nonsense for one day. Jack was in another of his damn moods. Maybe was just the Star Drive anxiety that hit everyone on board. Now that they were out of the Drive, Phil felt a lot better himself. You always forgot how bad it was. Phil had done it seven times before, but he'd never really gotten used to it.

The vacuums had already sucked up the fire-extinguishing gas, but as far as Phil could see there'd been no fire, just that huge plate blown off. Phil crouched in front of the Star Drive assembly and tried to think. Probably Number Six's pressure had backed up in the main power blower unit, and when that burst, the hyper accelerator piston had been flung through the resonance chamber, taking out the other primary thrusters and ripping off the chamber's cover plate. Phil was glad he'd come out of the Pod hatchway thirty seconds before the engine blew, as the heavy cover plate would've killed anyone it struck. As the entire crew descended on him, he noticed, with all the others, that the plate was embedded in the twisted remains of the escape craft's engines. "Damn ..."

"At least it didn't punch through the side of the ship, Phil," Joe said. "Besides, an escape craft isn't of much use in interstellar space."

"Connors, you find out where we are yet?" Jack demanded.

"Uh, no, Jack," said the slender, fair-haired Connors. "I've got the computer working on it."

"Well, get back up there and stick with it. If there are any problems, I want you on top of them instantly."

"Well, the computer's constantly checking it."

"Move it! You, too, James. Start monitoring any communications in this area. But we're not making any distress calls, got that?"

Those two moved to their stations. "Everyone wants to gawk like a buncha stupid jerks," Jack complained, glancing at everyone he deemed unauthorized viewers of the mishap. But besides Phil, only Borman and Joe were left. Phil could feel Jack's impatience burning onto his back as he inspected the half-melted gears in the resonance chamber. He'd heard Jack's fight with Borman over the intercom, and it hadn't been exactly Phil's idea of how top command operated. As far as he was concerned, Jack, Joe, and Lee were all unwanted at the engine.

"Yeah, it was Number Six all right," he said. "It backed up into the main blower. I would say the weakest point in the whole Star Drive design."

"The whole thing was stupid from the beginning," Jack said. "The *Typhoon* was always supposed to be a sublight *fighter-bomber,* not a damn Star Drive freighter! We could've *ferried* her over last July with no problem."

Phil was silent, poking with a screwdriver at various hot pieces of metal.

"Dammit, Sperry, did you hear me?"

Phil turned around. "Yeah, I heard you, man."

"I don't like the tone of your voice, Major."

Phil stood up. He was four inches taller than Jack. "Admiral, I don't like your tone, either. Would you please calm down? Can we all please go back to a first-name basis?"

"You're just like Borman here! A laggard, and undisciplined!"

"Dammit, Jack, would you grow up? You're a space captain, for God's sake! And you're head of the USSF! So why are you acting like a child?"

"I'm not acting like a child, damn you!"

Everyone went silent. Phil exchanged a glance with Borman, who shrugged. Joe inspected the floor. Sure, nobody had liked Lee's habit of getting sloshed the past few weeks, but Jack was definitely carrying things way too far, threatening Lee with a shattergun, then waving it at Phil himself.

"Would you mind explaining to me, Major Sperry," Jack snarled, "why your Thruster Six decided to blow, and why you were not at your station to tend to it?"

"Dammit, Jack! You blew off the Eight-Minute Check, the Ten-Minute Check, and the Fourteen-Minute Check! If you'd done your job properly we could've caught this in plenty of time! Plenty of time! I can't do a damn thing about the thruster pressures unless I have the data from the checks! Dammit to hell, Jack!"

"You were in the Pod, ignoring my orders to stay with your engine! You were helping Amav!"

"She needed it! We had to lash those Martians down to the coffee tables!"

"The hell she needed help! Because of your actions, Sperry, we're marooned in deep space!"

"We're *not* marooned. It was just Star Drive that blew. The Augmented Nuke is fine. We still have one-fifth light capability. Our internal systems--air pressure, artificial gravity--are fine. We've got full electrical power. We're okay."

"Joe, prepare court-martial papers for Major Sperry here.

And for Lieutenant Borman as well."

"Jack, you can't just court-martial the guy," Joe said. "Even if he wasn't at his post, it was really just an honest mistake. He was doing what he thought--"

"He was doing what he thought with my *wife!* I told him to leave her be!"

"Hoo-boy," Phil said. "Jack, you are really--"

Jack's hand was again on his shattergun.

"God, I thought it was just the Star Drive making him edgy," Borman commented. "But he really *is* nutso."

"Joe, are those court-martial papers ready yet?"

"*Jack ...*" Joe pleaded.

"Then consider yourself confined to the Pod. Draw up court-martial papers for yourself as well."

Connors and Patrick James clambered down the ladder from the catwalk and stood by them again. "Here's our position," Connors said, handing Jack his own comm.

"No radio signals detected," James added. "We're in the middle of nowhere."

"*Dammit ...*" Jack muttered. He distractedly scanned Connors' USSF Comm, then handed it to Joe.

At that moment Amav appeared along with the three Martians. Dar, the tallest, with the largest back fin, gave Phil a wide crinkly smile.

"Dar! I see you're feeling better!" Phil said. Of course, all seven humans could easily read the minds of Dar, Kner, and Fulr. The jagged patterns of suicidal anguish had been replaced with the serene mathematical beauty of Martian thought. As he stared into Dar's unlidded, two-inch-wide eyes, Phil was filled with empathy for the terror the Martians had undergone in Star Drive. He also understood their embarrassment upon recovery. Phil pulled back to survey all three Martian minds. The effect was that of hearing three radio stations at the same time, all playing eighteenth-century chamber music, but different works, different composers. But you could tune into one or the other as you wished.

Phil still couldn't believe he was standing here drawing on

the mental resources of beings over a thousand years old. How could he allow himself to be dragged under by Jack's petty anger?

And there was Amav. God, she was lovely. Tall, slender, just turned twenty-two, with that long dark hair, those luscious brown eyes, that perfect figure in a tight red jumpsuit. Why did Jack scorn her? Why did he act as if she were a burden? How could she be a burden? Every minute Phil had spent in her company the past few months had been ecstasy.

It had only been a month and a half since Phil realized he loved her. It had been at Jack's promotion party at Marsport USSF headquarters, and it had also been Amav's birthday. She sipped wine with Phil as the late afternoon Martian sunlight had filtered through the window and gone clear through her transparent blouse. God, how he'd ached for that perfect womanly body.

And after the party, when he was alone, heading for his car in the parking lot, he'd turned to catch the sun reflecting off the crimson sides of the United System Building. The beauty of that light was still fresh in his mind, the late afternoon sunlight on that rocky, empty, silent alien world. Their new home, Mars. And he'd told himself: *I love Amav.*

And dammit, ever since December 8th he'd struggled to deny that he was in love with this beautiful, sexy, delightful woman. As Jack stood in front of the Star Drive engine, clearly exasperated at the arrival of the entire crew, Phil gave Amav a little nod and received her little smile.

Could she possibly feel the same way? How could that be? She'd just married Jack in July. Incredible whirlwind romance, so everyone had said. And when those two were hitting it off, they seemed damn good together. And Jack had been a good friend for years. He was their leader, after all. How could Phil doubt his friendship, even if Jack was in this pissy mood?

He had to admit it. It was Jack that Amav loved. It was just that she was so friendly and open with everyone. Well, except maybe Borman. Somehow those two had irritated each other from the beginning. But in any case, it had to be that Phil was simply misinterpreting her natural good will.

Phil inspected the Star Drive. He'd been in love before, a couple of times, in his thirty years, but never like this. But hell, he wasn't supposed to be saying it was really love. Then what was it? Mere sexual desire? He stole another glance at Amav's breasts, her legs, her eyes. No, it wasn't just sex. Phil closed his eyes.

"The question is, where the hell are we?" Jack said. "This pile of crap here doesn't tell me much, Will." He snatched Connors' USSF Comm back from Joe and flipped it into Will's face. Will barely caught it. Phil was relieved that Jack at least had gone back to first names.

Will picked up on this gratefully as well, his former irritated, sardonic manner morphing into puppy-like devotion to Jack.

It was damn uncanny how Jack could turn that quality on and off in people. Hell, Phil could feel Jack doing it to him right now.

"Well, Jack," Will said, "it looks like we're about four months out of the Centaurian system."

"Four *months?*"

"God, man, are you kidding?" Borman put in.

"Quiet, Lee," Phil said gently, hoping to preserve the newfound civility.

"Four months at one-fifth light," Connors said, scanning his comm. "One hundred twenty-two days. Assuming that we can't get the Star Drive repaired. And I assume we can't," he added, looking over the shattered drive unit.

Phil shrugged. "You assume right. This thing is *totaled.*"

"Four *months?*" Amav said. "Will, are you sure you calculated it right?"

"I can't believe this!" Jack fumed.

Will turned to Amav. "Well, you do know that Alpha Centauri is 4.3 light years from Sol."

"Well, sure."

"Which is 25.278 *trillion* miles," Will explained.

"*Oh.*"

"I knew that," Jack snapped. "You'd think your average planetary engineer would, too."

"I do know it!" Amav protested. "It's just that we don't normally think in those terms."

"In any case, Star Drive allows us to make that in fifteen minutes," Will went on. "You could think of it as a little over 101 trillion miles per hour, but of course Star Drive's not actually traveling in normal space."

"Skip the lectures, Will," Jack said. "She doesn't need to understand any of that."

Amav opened her mouth, then shut it. Will punched more commands into his comm and eagerly continued: "If we traveled the entire distance to Alpha Centauri at our normal one-fifth light speed, it would take 21.5 years. So each minute we're in Star Drive is actually worth 1.4333 years at normal cruising speed."

"Crap! Crap!" Jack said.

"Star Drive failed at 14:46 into the journey. We needed just fourteen seconds to complete it."

"*Dammit!*" Jack fumed. "Fourteen *seconds?* Sperry, couldn't this piece of crap have held another *fourteen seconds?*"

But everyone ignored Jack, waiting for Will to spell it out. "The upshot is that, even with just fourteen seconds left, we still have 393.2 *billion* miles to go to Alpha Centauri. And that's 122.15 days at one-fifth light. Four months."

"Dammit to hell," Jack muttered, holding out his hand for the comm, which Will meekly turned over. Jack scanned it for a few seconds, finally entering some figures of his own. "*Dammit,*" he repeated, flipping it back to Will. "We were just too tired to be launching that late. We've all been on this ship twenty damn hours. Nobody can think straight. Then the damn Star Drive hit." He smacked a fist into his palm. "If the goddamn *media* hadn't held us up!"

"Hell, that came in the middle of the Arkonsky Relay glitch," Joe said. "We were all sitting around twiddling our thumbs by that point anyway."

"Huey Vespertine!" Jack spat. "That traitorous slob! Why

did I ever agree to that? He *shamed* us during the Hergs war, and now *this*."

"Why'd you let him? It was almost as much a disaster as when he interviewed us on the *Andromeda* last year."

"Hell, I guess I was trying to make amends, get some good publicity, I don't know."

Phil, involved with USSF technicians on the Star Drive's Arkonsky force field problem, had missed all but the last couple minutes of the corpulent Vespertine's AresNet interview, by which time Jack was screaming on AresNet that his old Naval Academy buddy, who'd been slickly prophesying doom for the *Typhoon's* peacekeeping mission to Alpha Centauri, was a vile traitor who should be *exterminated.* Jack's contrite apology, extorted by Huey live to the entire United System, hadn't helped matters. The Supreme Commander of the USSF should *not* have excused himself by saying "It's been a long day, and I guess we're all a little stressed."

"Hell, half the interview was Huey ruminating about what a piece that new wife of his is," Borman said. "I'd sure like to see a 3-D holo of the lady. Preferably the way Mr. Vespertine likes to see her." He jerked at Amav's glare. "Uh, sorry."

Joe shrugged. "She sure keeps herself out of the media. But I can't figure out why Huey still has to slobber on and on about her on every newscast. Hell, they've been married half a year, you'd think the thrill had worn off by now."

"Joe!" Amav mocked. "Maybe they're really in love!"

Love. Phil sighed. Amav knew about love, and passion, and keeping it alive through marriage. Could a traitor like Huey Vespertine have something to teach them all about passion? Or did Amav have something to teach *Phil* about passion?

"Sperry," Jack barked, "is the Star Drive really unrepairable?"

Phil shook his head. "Sorry, Jack. I could repair the unit myself, if I had parts. The thrusters are okay, but I'd need a new main blower, a new hyper piston, and a new resonance chamber, not to mention the cover plate and a host of minor parts."

"Don't we stock those?"

"We should have, Jack. I'm sorry. Nobody thought this would happen."

Jack frowned, but to Phil's relief didn't burst into fresh diatribes. "Okay. Let me think. Four months. Can we handle that? Do we have food?" As Phil nodded, Jack paced. "Okay. We need to get to Station One. We should've been there five minutes ago, according to the superspace message we radioed there at the Six-Minute Check. I only hope they don't conclude we've been shot down and launch some new offensive."

"It could've been worse," Connors said. "Let's say Star Drive had gone out, say, ten minutes in, or two-thirds of the way." He punched at his comm. "At one-fifth light speed, this would've left 7.1659 *years* to--"

"Okay, okay, Will, we get the damn point. That sort of speculation won't do any good."

"Thank God it came near the end," Amav said. "Maybe we can get the Star Drive repaired at Station One."

"Yeah, but what do we do if we finally get there and discover it's been blown to nothing? Then we're up the creek." Jack kept pacing. "Hell, we've got to do it, I guess."

"Four damn months," Borman muttered. "Cooped up like goddamn *animals*."

"We'll deal with it," Jack snapped. "We have to." He looked up and down the craft, at the smashed escape ship, at the blown Star Drive. Phil thought he detected a new cockiness in Jack's eyes. Yeah, Jack had probably felt a fifteen-minute Star Drive to another solar system was just a boring commuter trip. Now he had his sublight power and control again. Now he knew he could maneuver, he could see the stars, he could shepherd his ship through danger.

"Okay, first we need to send a superspace message to Station One," Jack said, then frowned.

Phil didn't have to elaborate for Amav's benefit, but Patrick James went ahead: "Superspace radio uses Star Drive, Jack."

"Yeah." Jack blew out some air. "Phil, any possibility of repairing just the superspace radio?"

Phil shook his head. "I'm sorry, Jack. We have to be *in*

superspace to send a superspace message. Unless we have one of those huge superspace modules like back at USSF HQ."

"Okay. Okay. First of all, we'll do a thorough inspection of the ship. And we'll test the Augmented Nuke before we open it up any faster. That explosion may have damaged something, never can tell. Phil, I want you to make sure the Star Drive is completely dismantled before we do another thing. I want the force field shut *down*."

"No problem, Jack. The computer's already done that for us. If it hadn't, the loss of pressure would've black-holed us instantly."

"Then we'd *really* be nowhere," Patrick James put in.

Jack grimaced. "Pat, I want you to be on special lookout for Centaurian spacecraft. I know we're a few months out of their territory, but you can't be too sure."

Pat took a sharp breath. So did Connors. Phil shared that feeling.

Only Will, Pat, Lee, and Phil had actually fought in Alpha Centauri, and Lee probably had to be discounted, as he'd turned the whole experience into a scoring game. But did anyone think Phil enjoyed his own turret experience? That he enjoyed taking life? Hell, here he was, an M.D., trained to use world-wrecking PlanetBlasters.

James and Connors shared that horror. Connors was the only person here who'd flown one-man fighters in combat, the only true fighter pilot among them. He'd been good, no doubt about it, 2,500 kills over a year's time. He looked a lot older than his twenty-seven years. The last month of his combat tour, which he'd spent marooned on an asteroid after he'd been shot down, had added to those years on his face, and was probably the reason he was now the *Typhoon's* navigation officer rather than a pilot.

Patrick James had also been through Alpha Centauri, though he wasn't a gunner like Borman or Phil. But as a computer technician James had proven his courage, and probably more importantly, his ability to hold his mind together, as he repaired complex systems under soul-shattering combat conditions.

Jack and Joe had never been to Alpha Centauri. They'd been damn brave in the Hergs war, but they were going to be shocked at the scale of combat in Alpha Centauri. Sure, when they dropped the Xon and ended the Final War, they'd killed more human beings than anybody in history. But that was just push-button combat. Still, Phil marveled that either of them had held together in the face of what they'd been ordered to do.

"Phil," Jack said, crouching down beside Phil at the engine, "do we still have cloaking technology?"

Phil consulted a panel. "Sure do. Of course, if we use it all the way in it'll slow us down some."

"We'll use it as the need arises. All right, men, back to your posts."

"Uh … Jack?" Borman stepped up after Joe, Pat, and Will left, ducking his head at Amav and the Martians as if wished them away as well. But nobody took the hint.

"Yeah, what is it, Lee?"

"God, Jack, I'm sorry for how I acted back there. I didn't really get, you know, drunk. I just had a sip or two, and all of a sudden the damn Star Drive hit."

Then Jack's charisma unfolded. It was always a dizzying experience, it broke down your resistance, and you forgot the tyrannical Jack. You only knew you'd follow this honest, experienced man anywhere. Jack looked Borman sternly in the eye, then grinned. "What the hell, Lee, we were both out of our gourds! I had no idea Star Drive could hit you like that!"

"Well, the more times you do it, it gets a little easier to take," Borman said, warming, in his dull way, to Jack's fire. "This was my ninth time, so I had some warning."

"Hell, Lee, look, I've heard that lots of people's nerves get a little unsteady during Star Drive. It's nothing to be ashamed about. Just don't try the booze again. Ask Sperry here for a couple tabs of DreamGlaze."

"Well, sure, Jack, I, uh, I sure am sorry."

Jack clapped an arm around Borman. "Don't worry about it, Lee. Like you were saying in your book, we men have got to stop acting so macho. If our nerves get unsteady during Star Drive, it's no crime! We can admit it! Next time I'm gonna get a few tabs of DreamGlaze myself. I had no idea the Drive packed that much wallop!"

Borman grinned. "Well, I guess I'll be gettin' to my turret now."

"Right. If Phil here needs some help, you can probably be of assistance. Phil, call Lee here if you need any help."

"Right," said Phil. He was happy. They were a family again. He didn't even mind when Jack moved off with his arm around Amav, hairy hand slapping her tight round bottom. Then Phil noticed that part of this feeling of universal benevolence came from the Dar symphony at full volume, uncluttered by other stations now that Kner and Fulr had returned to the Pod. The rest of the crew was off checking the first items on the Standard Inspection List. Dar was regal in his golden Martian Elder's Robe. "Hello," Dar beamed straight into Phil's head.

CHAPTER FOUR
The Dar Symphony

"Hello there," Phil replied. "I hope you three are feeling better."

"Yes, quite, thank you," Dar spoke aloud. "How are you?"

"Well, I just need to clear out this debris here, and make sure the Star Drive components are fully dismantled. Then I'll look over the Augmented Nuke." He smiled, realizing he hadn't answered Dar's question. "I'm fine. Maybe a little shook up by this."

Dar nodded. "I can see." Although the Martian Emperor tried to keep his next thought below the surface, Phil pulled it out anyway: *It must have been shocking to see your friend Jack behaving that way.*

Phil nodded. "Yeah, I guess it was."

Dar shrugged in embarrassment. A Martian wouldn't be ashamed to have his thoughts read by other Martians; more often than not they simply sat facing each other, exchanging data by telepathy, with a few ritual words spoken for aesthetic effect. All exchanged thoughts were fully understood by each. But a Martian was always surprised when a human being picked something out of his mind without the Martian being aware of it.

"Take it easy, Dar. The three of you were going through hell back there. I can see you're glad the Star Drive stopped."

"Yes, of course. I know it delays us, but if it had gone on even another five seconds, I don't think I could have withstood it." Dar spoke with his usual quiet nobility, but the images filling Phil's mind nearly dropped him to the floor: flames burning out Dar's central nervous system, accompanied by the graph of an exponential curve extending into infinity, mathematically documenting the progression of the pain.

"We had no idea it'd have that effect. I'll recommend we don't use the Drive until we get you safely back to Mars."

"That would be nonsense. I appreciate your concern, but none of you can afford a twenty-one-year trip back to Sol at our

31

present speed. If we can get the Drive fixed in Alpha Centauri, of course we'll use it to come home." He peered deeply into the demolished interior of the Resonance Chamber. "Of course, we Martians must be drugged unconscious before we do go back."

"Maybe you're right," Phil said. "But I don't relish causing you this discomfort."

"Speaking of discomfort, I'd like to change out of this Elder's Robe. The only reason I wore it was that I expected to be meeting senior Centaurian officials in a few minutes. But the Robe is intolerably tight."

The history of that particular robe surged into Phil. The Emperor's Robe first worn by the legendary K'Naaaar in the Great Polar War of Apocalypse. Stolen by the murderous Gluquffln in the Revolts of *K'nyuuggh'kk,* corresponding to the time of the building of the pyramids on Earth. Worn by Diuvwaln when he was assassinated during the Great Canal Controversy. Curiously, though no canals were ever built on Mars, despite the speculation generated by Earth scientists in the late 1800s, at about that time the Martians were debating whether or not to build canals on their planet, and Diuvwaln was killed as a result of his support for them.

Then there was one final image: Dar removing the robe in the presence of his young bride, the Empress, on their wedding night. K'sla remained on Mars, awaiting Dar's return.

As Phil shut down Star Drive subassemblies, Dar went on: "Of course I'm deeply concerned about the success of the mission. Jack's correct that an unexpected delay on our part, especially a four-month delay, could trigger unpleasant consequences."

Phil nodded. "Yeah, but there's nothing we can do about it now. We confirmed during the Six-Minute Check that Station One has already sent out peace feelers, and that we have a plenipotentiary personage coming to negotiate peace. Which of course is Jack, only they don't know that yet. I'm sure they'll have a fit when they find out it's the head of the USSF coming to talk peace. Jack wants to start negotiating, then reveal he's SCUSSF and that because of his recent appointment, the USSF is now for peace."

"It could well succeed. The Centaurians know they're gradually being worn down. And they'll respect a strong negotiator, one from the armed forces."

"I only hope Jack's up for it."

"Are you worried that because he's under stress, he won't be able to accomplish his task?"

"Uh, no, I didn't say that," Phil muttered. "What the hell, Dar? Are you learning to read *my* mind now? Of course that thought's crossed my mind. Jack's been driving himself and all the rest of us crazy the past few months. God knows where it'll all end."

"I only hope he can rise to the occasion. I'd hate to see him put Plan B into effect."

"God, yes." Plan B called for the black-holing of Alpha Centauri A, Alpha Centauri B, and Proxima Centauri, and the PlanetBlasting and Xon bombing of as many planets among the AC system's other stars as possible. Recently upgraded USSF translation systems to the major Centaurian languages held some promise for real communication, but they were still primitive. A year ago they'd had virtually no translation software. There were so many possibilities for misunderstandings.

"And by the way, I cannot read your mind, youngster!" Dar laughed.

"I sure hope not!" Phil grinned. He flushed the rad particles from the Star Drive waste collection subsystem into deep space and then opened that compartment with his wrench. Odd to think that if he'd opened it five seconds before, he'd have instantly killed everyone on the ship. The inner metal was still hot to the touch.

He was definitely glad Dar and the other Martians couldn't pry into his mind. Just how quickly would they figure out the curse of his lust for Amav? And then every other human on this ship would read Dar's mind in turn. Everyone would know. God, even Amav would know. Or did she know already?

It was unnerving how secrets kept popping out because of the Martians. Several times during the early weeks of mission preparation, each of the humans had gotten into a good long discussion with a Martian and, under the spell of the Martian's gentle honesty, said something that sooner or later was accessed out of the Martian's mind by everyone on the crew. Uncomfortable concepts bled out of the air: "I can't work with Connors. He gets *so* fussy." "I really think Pat's sitting on some bad emotional problems he refuses to face." "Hell, I don't know why Jack has to get so bent out of shape about it." "You'd think my crew could show a *little* more discipline." "I don't know why Lee's always cracking those stupid jokes about Amav." "Phil thinks he knows everything about this ship. Well, he sure as hell doesn't understand sensors. I'm sick of him messing it up." "Now that he's SCUSSF he thinks he's God."

But the crew adjusted. In fact, the airing of petty grievances solidified the team. But the humans quickly learned not to tell any Martians anything they didn't want their fellows to know. Naturally this grieved the Martians, since they were curious creatures. Phil's theory was that they'd evolved their telepathic powers from their intense curiosity to know each other. Oddly, this took the form not of being able to read other minds, but to send one's own thoughts outward.

They were especially curious about the "darkened house" of the human soul. Phil had picked that image out of Dar's thoughts: human minds as dark, boarded-up houses, which the curious Martian knocked at, sniffed, and put his ear up against. That these houses had loudspeakers mounted above the front door, broadcasting only select portions of the human mind in the form of oral discourse, frustrated the Martians even further.

The worst thing was that they had no concept of being lied to. They took everything at face value. Their nearest concept was self-delusion, an example being their disastrous worship of the usurper Hergs in the Martian war. The Martians simply couldn't accept that the human Hergs could distort the truth. It was no wonder that Martians were in awe of humans, whose darkened minds represented numinous power. That was probably why they'd fallen under Hergs' spell in the first place.

Often, to his shame, Phil would take advantage of Martian

curiosity by manipulating a conversation along certain paths, specifically the path of Amav. The problem in accessing information from the Martian mind was that, while current thoughts radiated forth without effort, Martian memories only entered that radiation flow in a happenstance manner, triggered by concepts or sense impressions that came up during conversation. So Phil would slowly shift the conversation to Amav, all the while pretending a purely objective interest in the subject. Before long hundreds of conversations Amav had had with Dar, Kner, or Fulr would float in front of him.

And images. Amav in scores of different outfits, standing, sitting, gesturing. But no Martian had ever seen her naked. Phil had been sure there'd be at least one image. No Martian had heard her talk about any attractions she might feel for other men. For Phil.

Phil could make little sense of some Martian memories. A Martian might attach an interpretation to an image of Amav that rendered it meaningless to Phil. And since memories triggered other memories, concepts could leap out that were so alien that Phil would physically cringe. A conversation about Amav's work on planetary engineering might pull up Martian soils, which might pull up the Tunnels of *Hlyyiathlrerr,* and the Wars of *Fmghfulf,* or Amav might pull up K'sla, and a particularly delicious afternoon of Martian sex, and Martian bathing customs after sex, and Martian tea ceremonies and Martian kitchens, and Martian mini-shatterguns used for cleaning kitchens, all without the Martian being aware that these memories were being accessed.

Unless the Martian was as sharp as Dar. One time Phil had tapped a memory of Dar and Amav arranging potted plants on her father's front porch in Alaska, and he'd been rewarded with a long, blissful video of Amav bending over in impossibly tight green pants, brushing back lustrous dark hair. Dar had been puzzled by Phil's enraptured gaze and asked if something about potted plants was especially appealing. "After all, for some reason I'm recalling the time Amav and I set out all those plants at Dr. Frankston's house."

"Uh, no, of course not," Phil stammered through an idiotic grin.

"Or perhaps it's the thought of Amav. You're such a good friend to her."

"Well, uh, sure. But maybe it *is* the plants. I do like plants, I guess."

"Interesting. I like plants too. Of course, we have no plants on Mars." Phil thought he'd caught a wary look from the Martian. Could Dar finally be learning to detect that great human social lubricant, the little white lie? Was he figuring out that Phil's innocent mentions of Amav in every conversation betrayed his passion for her? For a while Phil thought of going instead to Kner or Fulr, but realized in shock that Kner and Fulr knew everything Dar knew.

Then, to his dismay, he understood that any human on the *Typhoon,* including Jack, including Amav, simply had to mention the concept "Amav" to obtain from any of the Martians a long string of conversations between Dar and Phil on that subject. Maybe they were innocent conversations to Dar, but to the other humans, Phil's intentions could so easily be divined.

Was it true? Had everyone seen Phil's desire? For a week afterwards he tried to mention the other crewmembers to Dar the same way he'd mentioned Amav, trying to balance it out, make himself look like a curious ship's physician interested in all crewmembers. But then he saw that even that move would show up on the Martian Telepathic Bulletin Board, an abrupt absence of talk about Amav and unnatural talk about the rest of the crew.

He'd finally decided that the whole Martian mental network was too complicated for him or anyone else to sort out all those concepts. Everybody had to be overwhelmed by the thousands of ideas radiating from three Martian minds, and so no organized pattern of Phil talking about Amav was likely to emerge from the chaos. He resumed bringing up Amav in conversation with Dar, cautiously now, once again receiving a stream of images and thoughts about her.

Delicate work, to probe so slowly, so objectively, when sometimes it was all he could do to keep from screaming that he was out of his mind with desire for Amav Frankston-Commer. And why shouldn't Phil be allowed to confess everything to Dar? Wouldn't Dar be the perfect shoulder to cry on? Didn't he understand everything with his ancient alien wisdom? Wouldn't he eagerly soak up the story of Phil's love for Amav?

Damn you, Phil Sperry, for going ahead and falling in love like this!

Phil switched off the auxiliary current feeder, slammed the hydrogen plate back in place, angrily fed nuts to its twelve bolts, and ratcheted them tight.

"Is something the matter?" Dar said. "You seem preoccupied."

"Me? Hell, no! Naw! I'm just frustrated this shutdown is taking so long."

"Are you sure? It's as if you haven't heard a word I've said."

"Me? Hey, Dar, I've been listening, man, I've heard everything."

"I've been asking you repeatedly what you thought of the Centaurian Boundary Policy and yet you do not answer. You stare off into space as if preoccupied."

Phil grinned. "I bet you wish you could read my mind, don't you?"

Dar smiled. "It's merely a question of my not understanding you. Since I can't read your mind, I assume there's no need for me to do so. I know you're telling me the truth, of course. It's just that I don't always understand your human truth."

Phil winced. How could Dar be so smart and so stupid at the same time? Didn't he know that Phil harbored dire human truths he had to keep secret from everyone?

"Of course," Dar went on, "some of us have advanced the theory that Mind is to be thought of as that which radiates naturally, and thus the human mind must consist entirely of what you humans speak. That there's nothing more to you than what you say. Of course, I've learned to accept that there must be more there, somewhere in the darkened house."

"If you only knew," Phil muttered, realizing too late that

he'd let a little bit slip out. Now anybody on the crew could pick *that* little statement out of Dar's mind. And they had intuition even if Dar didn't.

But Dar went on gaily: "And that's where much of the misunderstanding first arose between Martians and humans. We probed, and simply could not find, a Mind beyond those first gruntings we heard issuing from your mouths. We even learned your main planetary languages, English and Chinese, but still thought of those as a simple code used to control your individual soldiers. We kept probing for Mind somewhere, finally assuming that it had to exist as some disembodied force back on your own planet. It was only after we started reading your books in your vast libraries, and talking with the wisest among you, that we began to have an inkling of the nature of your darkened house. It still remains unsettling to think of Mind being something which need not radiate. But we have decided we have much to learn from your young race."

Phil worked at the absorption generator relay, the final Star Drive component needing checking and a full shutdown. He tripped its main switches, counted thirty seconds by his watch, and began working off its two main valves.

Didn't Dar understand that even a human mind *must* radiate? Somehow? The Martians couldn't seriously think the darkened human house was some glorious mystery. Humans were trapped in there. They were terrified to come out. The Martians had nothing to learn from imprisoned cowards decaying in the stench of their own secrets.

Dar eyed him innocently.

What if Phil told him everything right now? About needing to take Amav into his arms? To kiss her? She returning it? The two of them dedicating their lives to each other? Yes, Phil would marry her, betray Jack, quit the USSF, quit everything. Jack was just a child who could never comprehend her, never fulfill her needs. But Phil would make love to Amav with all his passion, every ounce of his being. He'd never loved like this before. Never felt these feelings.

My life is Amav! I have to admit it!

Dar would understand it all. The darkened house would glow bright orange, and Dar would eagerly embrace the radiance, because the Martians knew everything about the relationship of male and female. Dar would help Phil get Amav away from Jack, counseling the ultimate woman, who'd undoubtedly be a bit dazed by the whole process, that her real destiny lay with Phil. Phil's desire for her must have been obvious all along, and therefore, surely she had the same desire for him.

That's all it would take. One big confession. Dar would broadcast the secret of Phil's soul to everyone on board. And why not? Why the hell not? Why not communicate that, *radiate* that, for the first time in his life? Maybe it didn't even matter if Amav ever came to him. Maybe Phil's entire life was a tragedy. Well, so what, at least he'd *radiate*. At least, at last, he'd be a total human being.

"Dar … *Dar!*" Phil flung down his screwdriver and embraced the astonished Martian.

"Philip! Whatever is wrong?"

"Nothing's wrong! Nothing! Dar, there's something I've got to tell you!" He peered into Dar's giant, mild violet eyes and was overwhelmed by images of Amav: Amav looking up to Dar, earnestly seeking some wisdom, some higher understanding from the great Martian. Dar was playing back thousands of memories of Amav at her most beautiful and most honest. Had he subconsciously understood what Phil needed to say? Had Dar pieced it all together by himself?

"Something--you need to tell me?"

"No! I mean yes! Or God! Maybe I shouldn't! Maybe--"

It seemed his own scream was echoing throughout the *Typhoon II,* but as Phil clutched Dar's wrists in amazement, he realized it was the alert siren wailing at shattering volume. And Jack's shriek came on the line:

"Attention all hands! Red alert! Red alert! James has just sighted a spaceship 4,000 miles ahead! Configuration-- Centaurian!"

CHAPTER FIVE
The Limits of Three-Martian Amplified Thought

"Borman, Sperry! To your blasters!" Jack barked. "One Xon bomb--armed!"

Dar felt his pulse race from the strain in Jack's voice. "Jack!" Phil shouted next to him. "Want me to man the Xon console up there?"

"Negative! Joe and I will handle it! I want two turret men on this!"

Scattering his tools, Phil ripped open the plastiglass hatch to the upside-down ventral turret. It was so rare to touch a human being, and at those moments Dar felt on the verge of being able to read more from the human's mind than these humans ever spoke. And Phil had wrenched loose of a fascinating new contact. He'd been about to reveal something in his darkened soul, something Dar had never suspected.

"Ready for maximum acceleration on my command!" Jack yelled.

Halfway into his turret, Phil hit his intercom and shouted: "Jack! Wait! I never had time to check the Augmented! We can't be sure that the Star Drive explosion didn't jar something loose!"

"Inspection in Navigation isn't complete yet either!" Connors said.

"The hell with Navigation! I just ordered inspections to keep us busy! But we don't have time! If we have to blast that Centaurian, we just have to!"

"Jack, if you can give me a minute, I'll check the main power turbo!" Phil said. "It's the major component shared with the Star Drive, and it might've been damaged!"

"To your turret, Major! Okay, Joe, let's go for it!"

Dar stepped back as the Augmented Nuclear Reactor to the left of the dismantled Star Drive surged into life. Its gathering hum was accompanied by a growing yellow radiance from the transparent matter tube. Dar shielded his eyes, which were a hundred times more sensitive to light than human eyes.

Phil started for the turret, hesitated, and turned back to the ship's engines.

"Speed 10,000 miles per hour," came Joe's voice. "14,000--16,000--"

"Closing on target," said Patrick James.

"Dorsal blaster set to Centaurian configuration," Borman called. "Maximum power loading *now.*"

"Speed 22,000 ... 24,000," Joe called. "Hold! We have warning light! Warning light! Blaster energy drain! Borman, shut down your blaster!"

Phil flung himself on the Augmented Nuke. "Dammit! Dammit! Power turbo--no pressure! The lifters are probably scored to hell!" He pulled down a big red switch. The humming and the yellow brilliance vanished. Several lights went out, then slowly powered up as the storage batteries kicked in. Dar noted a significant lessening of the artificial gravity.

"Goddammit! Sperry, why the hell did you shut my nuke down?" Jack snarled. The hatch to the Control Room burst open and Jack bounded down the fuselage past the wrecked escape ship.

Phil whirled. "Because we lost coolant pressure to the power turbo, which would've blown us to bits in another ten seconds, but also to the reactor itself! God help us if we melt down!"

"Are we gonna melt down? Huh? Huh?"

Phil scanned a panel. "Reactor temperature 5,043 degrees. It's iffy, Jack. Uranium dioxide melts at 5,189."

"Damn, what can we do? Sperry, how could this happen?"

"I just don't know. We just hit it with too much power, and probably the power turbo lifters were scored when the Star Drive froze up."

"It was my PlanetBlaster that did it," Lee Borman's voice came over the intercom. "I'm sorry, Jack. I screwed up again, I guess."

"God, who cares?" Jack said. "Sperry, we'll have to jettison the nuke!"

"It's my fault," Borman went on. "Jack, I'll kill myself, okay? I'll use my shattergun. Right now. I'm so sorry!"

"Borman, belay that! I specifically forbid you to kill yourself! Is that clear?"

"Well, Jack, if you say so ..."

"God, what a zoo. Joe, are you there? Activate jettison program! Everyone away from the back of the ship!"

"Jack, we have to be wearing *spacesuits* for that!" Phil said. "We don't have the damn time!"

"We'll all go to the Control Room and pressurize it! Have you got any other suggestion, Sperry?"

"We don't *know* if it'll melt! Maybe--"

"No time! No time! Everyone to the Control Room!"

"If you'll excuse us," Dar said, motioning Kner and Fulr forward. "Would you humans please keep your voices down?"

"What? *What'd* you say to me?" Jack shouted.

"We need quiet." Dar turned to Phil. "This mass of metal here?"

Phil brightened. "The reactor? Of course, it's this assembly right here. This boxy thing." Dar regarded the cube three feet on a side behind other boxes, tubes and wires. He felt for Kner and Fulr's minds to either side of him. He let himself drift, resonating on the same frequencies as his comrades.

Activate Amplified Thought Program, Dar commanded.

Activated, came Kner and Fulr's responses.

In harmony with his fellows, Dar felt for the chamber in front of them, felt its heat, its atomic reactions. Some of the metal was indeed beginning to bubble. He and Kner and Fulr, with the exhilarating sense of thought processes stepped up to hundreds of times normal strength, set to work on the uranium dioxide inside the chamber.

"Reactor temperature--fifty-seven degrees?" Jack said in disbelief.

"Total shutdown," Phil said. "Control rods inserted. No reactions taking place."

Dar opened his eyes. Kner and Fulr blinked and smiled.

"Well, thanks, Dar!" Jack said. "And Kner, and Fulr! You saved the ship!"

Dar shrugged. "It's really nothing."

If only Amplified Thought could penetrate into the unreadable interiors of these human minds! What treasures must be there!

"So I see you finally did perfect the Three-Martian Amplified Thought Program," Phil said. "That's amazing!"

"We worked out the final subroutines in the last couple weeks." This had been a sore point with the USSF. The main architecture of Three-Martian AT, a major advance over the existing 500-Martian Amplified Thought program, had been developed last summer, but many of the subroutines hadn't been connecting properly. Dar, Kner, and Fulr, along with several hundred Martian mind programmers, had only been able to write the final draft of the program two weeks ago. Some of Dar's radical proposals, including a rough theory of "minds choosing not to radiate," had been the turning point in overcoming the bugs in the software.

If the program hadn't been ready, there wouldn't have been any point in sending three Martians on this journey. Jack had been upset up to launch time about the need to carry three extra passengers in the hope that their untested program would work.

"Why didn't you guys tell me you could do this?" Jack said. "Would've saved us all a lot of trouble."

"Well, we tried to tell you last week, but you appeared to be too busy to meet with us. We hoped you'd just be able to read our thoughts on the matter."

"Huh. Sorry, I must've missed it. But look, Dar, if you can freeze a reactor like that, suppose you three just get to work and rebuild both the Augmented Nuke and the Star Drive? Meanwhile we can defend ourselves with battery power on the turrets if those AC's get close. Can't vaporize 'em, but we can sure punch some holes in 'em."

"Well, our cloaking's gone, that's for sure," Phil said.

"Jack, this is Pat," came the voice over the radio. "We've missed the Centaurian. We're still drifting at 26,500 miles per hour, but the Centaurian's been holding steady at 25,000 and now we're off in two different directions."

"They showed no signs of engagement?"

"No, it's like they're dead. My sensors didn't pick up any unusual readings. They haven't varied their course an inch. Just drifting by. We got within 750 miles of 'em at closest approach. Distance is now 9,900 miles."

"Huh. What's he crawling around at 25,000 for?" Jack wondered, then turned to Dar. "Well, who cares? If you'll all get to work on the engines, I'll be heading back to the Control Room." He moved off, bouncing oddly in the low gravity.

"Jack," Dar said, "I'm afraid we'll be of no use in repairing your engines."

Jack whirled. "What? You won't repair my engines? Why?"

"Not that we would not, if we could. But we simply cannot."

"But you froze the chamber down! I saw that! I thought you guys said you could do anything with Amplified Thought!"

Dar frowned. He hated it when humans got unpleasant. He took a gulp of overly-rich human air and steadied himself. Surely Jack could read his mind and know the answer, but when humans were upset, they had difficulty reading the Martian outradiance. So Dar patiently explained: "Yes, we can do anything with Amplified Thought, if we know *how*. Amplified Thought gives our minds almost unlimited power, for instance, if we were within a few hundred thousand miles of a planet, Kner, Fulr, and I could cause it to explode." He frowned at the thought. "That's because destructive acts are fairly easy to accomplish, or simple actions, like lowering the temperature of the metal in that reactor."

"And?" Jack snapped, obviously still unwilling to peer further into Dar's thoughts. A pity, as Dar could have shown him all the mathematics in one grand sweep. As it was, he had to work to get the concepts across in spoken, linear fashion.

"So, if we have expert guidance from an authority on the subject, for example Amav's knowledge of planetary engineering, we can use the Thought constructively to build whatever we wish, to repair whatever we wish, to change or augment any object in the universe according to the desired plan. Destruction is easy. You just focus on the nuclei of atoms and start wrenching them this way and that until the energy spills out. Creation, on the other hand, implies the ability to think attentively and logically for long periods of time."

Jack dazedly shook his head. "Well, then, Sperry here understands the engines. Talk to him and do what he tells you."

Dar turned to Phil. "Is that possible? I thought the destruction was too intense."

"Not with the Augmented Nuke," Phil said. "We have spare parts for that, and fresh uranium rods. I even have a spare reactor kit in storage if we need it. I could use a little help there, maybe. I'm sure I can have the Augmented Nuke back up in a day or two. But as for the Star Drive, forget it, I don't have the parts."

"Well, hey, just ask these guys to make some parts," Jack said, pointing at Dar.

"It wouldn't work. I'm sure I could get the operating manual out and point to a picture of the part, and Dar and Kner and Fulr could fuse together a piece of metal that looked exactly like that part. But consider all the specifications for that piece of metal, the exact mixtures of all its alloys, the tolerances, all that stuff. That piece of metal would function just long enough to put Star Drive into black hole mode. I'm sorry, Jack. You know it can't be done."

Jack sighed. "Yeah, I know. Well, at least we'll have our normal drive again. Dar, will you and Kner help Phil repair the nuke?"

"Certainly."

"All right, then, let's get back to stations." He punched the intercom again. "Pat, anything new on that AC ship?"

Pat's voice cracked back: "I was just fixing to tell you, Jack. I just picked up an SOS from the thing. Only that, and nothing more, in Standard Space Code."

"Why would Centaurians be using SSC? What do you think, Phil?"

"Maybe they're playacting," Phil mused. "Let us think they're in trouble, then send out a USSF code. I don't know."

"Well, we sure can't turn around and follow it now. Not on batteries. But I have to admit I'm intrigued by the whole thing."

Dar cleared his throat. "Well, we Martians may be of

assistance here."

Jack turned to him. "What do you mean?"

"That ship isn't too far away," Dar said. "Kner, Fulr, link up with me now. Ah, yes, can you feel it?" Fulr and Kner nodded. Once the three Martians reentered the Amplified Thought program they could feel the mass and motion of the other ship. So for that matter could any human reading their minds.

"Prepare to grab it," Dar said. He turned to Jack. "Of course, matters of inertia aren't the strong point of Three-Martian Amplified Thought, and unfortunately we're already somewhat exhausted by cooling down the reactor. Dragging that Centaurian vessel back here will be almost at the limit of our capacities."

"Really?" Jack said. "But you guys blew up the gas giants with Amplified Thought! What about throwing Pluto clear out of the solar system with AT?"

Dar frowned. "Well, of course that's a long and painful story. Let's just say that the early versions of Amplified Thought, using five hundred Martians linked in a series, had a great deal of trouble with the concept of *inertia*."

"Huh. You got that right!"

Dar had no idea why Jack was so callous. Surely all the humans were reading the three Martians' dismal guilt at these failures.

"Well, it was a tremendous learning experience," Fulr put in. "And fortunately there was no life on those planets we accidentally destroyed."

"Quiet," Kner said. "We need to deepen the links on subroutine 455."

But Dar wanted to make sure Jack understood. "It was so easy to simply destroy when we were trying to *move* something. We needed raw materials. We wanted to build what you would call a Dyson sphere around the sun. But everything we touched we destroyed! With the 500-Martian program, even one Martian daydreaming could warp the efforts of the other 499."

"Jupiter and Saturn blowing simultaneously! A leftover

subroutine from the Neptune disaster! Unforgivable stupidity!" Fulr put in.

"We need to concentrate!" Kner hissed.

"Guys, is this really going to work?" Jack said.

"It will work," Dar said. "The bottom line is that Three-Martian AT simply doesn't have the power of the 500-Martian version. We keep refining it, but--" He shrugged. "Coordinate axis Z-1, call X55B."

"X55B called," Kner grunted. "Got it."

"The ship masses 3,940 tons," Fulr said. "Our combined speed difference is 51,500 miles per hour."

"What I'm saying, Jack," Dar went on, even as most of his brain calculated the energies necessary to grasp the alien ship, "is that inertia is not our forte. Otherwise, we could transport our own ship easily at near-light speed all the way to Alpha Centauri. But the fact remains that Three-Martian AT is quite limited in its power."

"Wait a second," came Joe's voice over the intercom. "Are you guys really gonna drag that Centaurian back to us?"

"Why not? It's giving a distress signal, and Jack said he's intrigued."

"Possibly beings on that ship are suffering," Fulr said. "Although I cannot read their minds."

"There are ..." Kner strained. "Between eight and ten *beings* aboard."

"Great," Joe called down. "Suppose they sling a meson bomb at us when you drag 'em alongside?"

"Why, they'll just blow the AC's up at the slightest sign of trouble, won't you, Dar?" Jack laughed. "I tell you, Joe, I didn't consider all the angles of AT! We don't need Xon bombs or blasters! We'll just point the Martians here at 'em and--zap!"

"Of course," Dar said hastily, wondering if Jack had heard a word about the limits of Three-Martian Amplified Thought, "we Martians do not wish to destroy."

"It would be easy for us to simply melt and seal off any launching tubes or other weapons," Kner put in. "We can easily neutralize any weapons."

Jack thought. "Okay, guys, go for it."

Dar arranged Kner and Fulr to either side and they stepped up the amplitude of their thoughts, focusing on that distant ship moving further and further away. With a distinct jolt the three locked their minds like a giant fist around the cylindrical hull of the Centaurian ship and began to drag the thing backwards. Dar was mildly surprised to realize that the task was much more difficult than he'd conceived. It took all of their strength just to reduce that craft's speed to zero. But the *Typhoon* was still moving away from the AC ship at 26,500 miles per hour.

Dar looked over at Kner and Fulr, who both shook their heads, dazed.

"Wow," Phil said. "You guys look trashed out. Maybe you'd better sit down."

"No, we will be able to continue. One moment, please."

Patrick James called down: "Distance: 19,670 miles."

"They must be dead," Jack said. "They allowed themselves to be reduced to zero velocity and haven't done a thing. I bet their SOS is just a computer talking to itself."

"Just leave it," Joe called down. "Let 'em rot right there."

Dar couldn't explain why he was so shocked at the thought of a spacecraft just sitting in space, with zero motion in respect to the rest of the universe, if such a concept had any meaning. At 25,000 miles per hour, the ship would at least have been going somewhere. At least *someday* it would plunge into a sun. That would probably take billions of years, but at least the ship had a journey to make. Besides, the beings on the ship were still alive. They had a right, even though they probably knew they were marooned, to feel that fate would take them somewhere.

"So," Jack said, picking up these thoughts, "you're thinking they're still alive? And you want to try again to bring them alongside?"

"Y-yes …" Dar said. The thought of the effort required was numbing. But he felt Kner and Fulr merge into his mind again and they reopened Amplified Thought. This time, the creative Kner had found a way to wrap energy fields in spirals of ever-increasing tightness, thus concentrating the force on the ship.

Dar pumped more energy into the new spirals, and found a way to relax his grip on the ship itself as he did so. *Yes, the IF-THEN statement in line 344,555 could be modified to an IF-THEN-ELSE, giving us the option of an Amplified Spiral Procedure utilizing a four-dimensional array.*

"Distance 20,560 miles," James called down. "And holding steady."

"You've matched us!" Joe said. "You've accelerated them to our speed!"

"Great work, guys!" Phil said. "Are you sure you're okay?"

Dar nodded. He could see the concern on Phil's face. Reading facial expressions on humans, in fact, the whole human science of body language, had only come to Dar after months of study. Kner and Fulr had never mastered it. Nevertheless, human body language offered the only nonverbal aid to the interior of the human mind, and Dar had always been eager to make use of it. Even Jack seemed to be registering concern amid all his bellicose stress.

"So how many Centaurians did you say were on that ship?" Jack said.

"I can't tell yet," Fulr said. "We still think eight to ten. Of course, the ship's further from us than it's been in all this time. But it should be fairly easy to reel it in now."

As it turned out, "fairly easy" became another twenty-one minutes of agonizing effort as the Martians, already exhausted by the first two pulls, sent out their Amplified Thought across 20,560 miles and once again took up the slippery inertial grasping at the object, accelerating it for a time to over 60,000 additional miles per hour.

At 2,000 miles the Martians got a sense of the outline of the ship and began melting and sealing various holes on the sides. Were these bomb launching tubes, or could the Martians be sealing up atmospheric ramjets? Were there other types of weapons they were missing? Dar caught Jack's grimace. Evidently Jack had picked this thought out of the Martians' heads.

So the three Martians proceeded to melt the entire surface

of the AC ship, reducing its hull to a seamless slag of gray metal.

"There are nine aboard," Kner said. "And they are all ... *human beings.*"

CHAPTER SIX
R'mrel'lasktm'uu

"Are you kidding me?" Jack said.

"Distance 1,000 feet," James called down.

"I've had it visually for a while," Joe said. The *Typhoon's* Control Room had the best view of outer space on board the ship, so Jack, Phil, and the three Martians went back up there. Amav joined them.

Joe positioned the *Typhoon* to get the best view of the floating hulk. Dar, Fulr, and Kner halted the other ship thirty feet from the *Typhoon's* nose.

"Relative velocity zero," Dar announced, cutting off Amplified Thought with a sigh.

"Why don't you three just sit down for a bit?" Phil suggested.

"Thanks. I think … I'll just sit right here …" Dar folded his legs beneath himself on the Control Room floor. Kner and Fulr did the same.

"No more inertia," Phil said. "That almost wiped you guys out."

"We'll recover … and we'll modify the Three-Martian AT program so we can handle tasks like these."

"So how are we going to get those people out of there?" Amav said. "We've melted any hatches completely shut."

Jack stiffened and whirled. "Amav, don't you have inspections to make in the Pod?"

"Well …" She pointed to the alien ship. "I just thought …"

"I know, I know, everyone wants to gawk. But we've got to have discipline on board. Back to the Pod, Amav, and I mean now!" Amav shrank back, then disappeared into the fuselage.

"Jack, honest to God," Phil said. "Anybody would be curious about that ship."

"You're out of line, Major. We're in the presence of an enemy vessel. I must have discipline."

"In that case, I'll return to my station at once."

"Sit still, Major. I have some duties for you here."

51

Dar was still in shock at Jack's treatment of Amav. The concept of "trouble between men and women" was alien to him. In the Martian culture one only fell in love once, though it could come anytime. Dar's own Love-Falling had come when he was 1,855 years old, fairly late by Martian standards. Whereas K'sla was only 344, probably the average age for Love-Falling. Once the Love-Falling had begun, the two lovers accelerated madly towards each other, reading each other's soul with ever-increasing understanding in preparation for the Great Erotic *J'thath*.

One school of Martian thought, the *F'yskimuyhf,* maintained that the purpose of falling in love was to bring one deeper and deeper toward the Final Truth of One's Being, and, when you had at last encountered the Final Truth, you died right there. Ceased to exist and were happy to, because after the Final Truth, why bother with anything else?

But Dar didn't accept the *F'yskimuyhf.* He sided with the *R'mrel'lasktm'uu,* which maintained that one fell ever deeper into infinite worlds of delight, that there was no need of any arbitrary Final Truth, that the only limit to one's lifespan was the limit of one's curiosity. Dar had declared to K'sla that the two of them would be the first Martians to live forever.

So Dar was quite disturbed at Jack's recent harshness towards Amav. At first he'd been sure Jack had a human version of *R'mrel'lasktm'uu* buried within him, but after seeing Jack's increasingly short-tempered treatment of Amav, he'd come to doubt that. And all Amav had done, really, was act like a regular crewmember on board Jack's ship, express her opinions forthrightly, and refuse to back down when Jack ordered her about. Unless, as just now, she evidently got what humans called "hurt" and left on the verge of tears.

Was something amiss between them? To a Martian, that concept was impossible. Yet from a perusal of human books, movies, and conversations, Dar had learned that mistaken *J'thath* was extremely common in Earth culture. So common that it seemed to be the rule rather than the exception. In fact, *J'thath* on Earth, as evidenced by that absurd book written by

Lee Borman, was so misunderstood and abused that it seemed to Dar that its primary purpose was to humiliate and degrade its practitioners.

What was more boggling was that mistaken *J'thaths* might eventually lead to true Love-Fallings, and true Love-Fallings could be marked by episodes of disharmony and mistaken *J'thath*. This had to be a result of the human inability to either radiate or read Mind.

Dar had hoped that Jack and Amav, perhaps as a result of his own presence, would overcome the merely human and embrace a pure *R'mrel'lasktm'uu*. But he'd nearly gone to pieces the first time he saw them arguing one August night at the USSF base in Alaska. Horrified, he'd assumed their *J'thath* was broken. Then, seeing them laughing and playing the next day, Dar had been thoroughly confused. This cycle had gone on and on, and Dar had to admit he'd grown somewhat used to it. That is, until December, when the bad times, what Dar thought of as "Cesspool *J'thath*," started outweighing the good. Who was to blame for the crime of polluting the Love-Falling? Dar loved both Amav and Jack. He felt he could understand Amav's pain, just as he could understand Jack's own stress and pain. Yet it was clear that Jack was the aggressor. He seemed to want to both deliver pain as well as experience it himself.

Of the humans, only Phil seemed to concern himself with the fact of the Cesspool *J'thath*. Phil spoke about Amav often, obviously trying to figure out ways to soothe Amav and Jack. Why else would Phil be so concerned for her? He had to care about her pain in a special way. Dar smiled. That was good. That was what friends were for. Amav was lucky to have Phil for a friend. So was Jack, for that matter.

This is Kner, came the voice in Dar's mind. *Code 14.*

Well! Dar thought in vexation. He'd done it again, forgetting that the very wondering about something amiss between Jack and Amav was bound to be pulled out by any of these humans, who apparently needed to keep these matters "secret" from each other. Dar still didn't understand what "secret" meant, but he knew he'd embarrassed his friends again.

He tried to control his thoughts, but since most humans could read his mind at a distance of a thousand feet, this meant that, in order to accommodate the human desire for "secrecy," a Martian had to control his thoughts at all times.

This was clearly the opposite of freedom, not even being able to think whatever you pleased. It was a violation of *R'mrel'lasktm'uu.* Yet at the same time it pained Dar to think that Joe and Jack and Phil, and probably Patrick and Will and Lee and Amav, had read that entire last series of thoughts along with Kner's Code 14, which was intended to tell Dar he was leaking thoughts again. Of course, saying Code 14 was stupid in itself, because the humans easily saw what it stood for: *Shut up, because these immature humans are going to get all upset again because they can see what you're thinking about them. And isn't Jack being petulant today anyway?*

Jack stared angrily at his feet. "I'm sorry, Jack," Dar whispered.

Jack did the human thing, looking away and pretending Dar hadn't spoken. "Okay, here's what we're going to do. Phil, you and I are going outside in suits with tether lines to help those people out of there." He turned back to Dar. "You're sure those are humans in there?"

"Yes. We can only feel for shapes in the Amplified Thought mode, and of course we can't read the thoughts of those humans, but we can follow their shapes. And, of course, you can read our minds and see those shapes as well." Exhausted as he was, Dar slid his mind into Kner's and Fulr's. They picked up a mild AT subroutine set to probe and nothing more. With a sense not exactly visual but more like radar, they built up a picture of nine beings clustered near the center of the ship.

"I can see 'em. Sort of. Okay, here's what we do. Are they picking up your minds?"

"I cannot say. From their movements, one might deduce ..."

"And then again, one might not," Kner put in.

"Here's what you do," Jack said. "Tell 'em to put spacesuits on, all nine of 'em. Tell 'em to have the suits on in ten minutes, because they're about to lose all their air."

Dar nodded, puzzled. But all three began concentrating on the concept of putting spacesuits on. The images in the ship started moving wildly.

"It's insane!" Joe said. "They're going berserk!"

"Yes, they do seem to be putting on garments," Dar said.

"Yes, that's a helmet. One of them just put a helmet on," Phil said.

"Weird helmets … weird shapes," Joe said. "God, Jack, I think they're putting on *Centaurian* spacesuits."

"Maybe they hijacked that ship," Jack said. "So all they'd have is Centaurian suits. I don't know. But they're human. They're our people. They were sending out the SOS, so I imagine they're freaked out."

"And they probably don't understand that the orders to put the suits on are coming from us," Dar put in.

"That's right. They're probably freaking out of their skulls," Joe said. "All of a sudden, this command to *put suits on* takes over in their minds."

"Phil, you and I had better get our own suits on," Jack said. "Joe, seal all compartments, both weapon turrets, and the Pod." He spoke into the intercom: "Amav, you in the Pod?"

After a long silence, a tiny: "Yes …"

"We're sealing it off from the ship for a few minutes. We're depressurizing the main cabin so Phil and I can go out. We need to keep the rear airlock completely open to get all nine of these people in fast."

"Well, be careful …" It was obvious she'd been crying.

"Dar! Have every person on board that ship who's got his life support up and running to raise his left hand."

Dar kept broadcasting that command in conjunction with Kner and Fulr until they got nine left hands held high. He was so intent on transmitting that command that he didn't notice the whoosh of main cabin depressurization, and he was surprised to see the bright white, red, and blue figures of Jack and Phil moving out from the *Typhoon* towards the Centaurian vessel. They attached a score of tether lines to the other ship.

"Okay, Dar," came Jack's voice over the radio. "Now drill

me a few very small holes, away from those people. Let their atmosphere leak out slowly. We don't want any explosions. And balance 'em so the ship doesn't move. I don't want my tether lines all tangled up."

The three Martians drilled the holes. Finally Dar said: "There's no air left in there, Jack."

"Fine. Now burn me a nice big hole in the side of this thing."

In seconds a slab twelve feet on a side fell away from the ship. And then nine figures, clad in bulky, ten-foot-high mustard-colored spacesuits, began to spill out of that hole. Their giant clear helmets, shaped to fit the huge tentacle-bearing heads of the Zarj Centaurian subspecies, showed human faces.

"Come on! Grab the lines! Don't trust those suit thrusters!" Jack kept calling as Phil demonstrated how to clutch at the lines and pull toward the *Typhoon*. "Aw, what the hell? They can't hear me. C'mon, grab the lines! C'mon!"

Joe said: "Damn, do I have a headache."

"I do too," came Will Connors over the intercom. "I have a feeling that our reading the Martians when they're doing Amplified Thought could do that."

"It very well could," Dar said. "We were making you people read things in a more tactile sense than you ever do with normal telepathy." He sighed. "I'm finished with AT for a few days myself. My headache must be a lot worse than yours."

"No, *mine's* worse than yours," Jack spoke over the radio. "But I won't ask you Martians to vaporize this ugly ship. We'll just let it drift." The rescued humans in the alien suits disappeared under the wing of the *Typhoon*. "Well, I think we saved us some people," Jack added just before he also sank out of view.

CHAPTER SEVEN
Refugees

Dar was happy to see Jack more his old relaxed self than he'd been in months. Perhaps the excitement of rescuing the newcomers had restored his sense of purpose. Jack was the perfectly genial ship's captain and host to the newcomers. He stood with Amav at his side, patting her and cajoling her back to cheerfulness.

He'd let the entire crew abandon their stations aboard the *Typhoon* for the Central Meeting Room on the Pod. Dar was glad to be back in the Pod's Martian gravity. Though he, Kner, and Fulr could adapt to human environmental conditions, they preferred to relax in their own environment whenever possible. Thus the Pod was kept at .38G. Though for safety reasons this main room was supplied with the human's thick atmosphere, the Martians could adjust any of the private compartments or the main negotiation rooms to Martian air and pressure.

The nine newcomers slumped in bright red armchairs on one side of the circular room, with the seven *Typhoon* crewmembers and the three Martians opposite. To the right was the spiral staircase, with the delightful adjustable gravity controls Dar never tired of playing with, leading back up into the *Typhoon*. The newcomers were so fazed by their rescue that they weren't even up to the simple task of dumping the Martians' thoughts into their minds and getting a full picture of the *Typhoon* mission, its current problems, and the way their own craft had been saved. They clearly weren't in awe of the Martians. They'd probably been in contact with dozens of alien species in the AC system, and were used to dealing with creatures that could scarcely be called Alpha Format, or, as the humans liked to put it, "humanoid."

Dar had to admit this group of humans didn't impress him. They seemed stringy and malnourished, their eyes blackened and blank. There were five men of varying ages, three women, and a preadolescent boy. Two of the men, Carl Rogers and Nathan Pollard, both in their late twenties, dressed in T-shirts and unshaven, seemed to be the spokespersons for the group. There was a fiftyish man, Ben McCasland, and his young wife Sheila. Dar got the impression that Ben would have been the leader under other circumstances, but had deferred to Rogers and Pollard. Another married couple consisted of Arbold Protor, who struck Dar as a loutish alcoholic in his mid-thirties, and his wife Catherine, who seemed sluttish and rumpled. A dumpy, nondescript woman named Anna Dorch and a shallow college-age man, Emory Bell, completed the cast of adults.

Dar didn't know why these people rubbed him the wrong way, for the usual Martian attitude was to welcome newcomers with an open heart. Only the twelve-year-old boy, Bobby Athens, struck Dar as at all pleasant. Dar noted that both Kner and Fulr shared these feelings.

"Your damn Martians don't like us," Carl Rogers snarled, sprawled horizontally in his chair. "I've heard talk you can read their minds. They don't want us on your ship, even though you blather all this crap about welcoming us."

"Well--" Jack choked. He glared at Dar. Of course, all the humans on board could read Dar's distrust of the newcomers. It was just that the newcomers, finally getting used to the fact that they'd just been taken off their own ship, were just starting to read the Martians. "I'm sure the Martians welcome you as much as we. It's just that they're a little paranoid in new situations sometimes," he lied. Mistake, because all Dar had to do was note the inaccuracy, and then Rogers and the rest could read that out of Dar's mind.

"Well, I share their views," Rogers said. "I don't like Martians at all. I don't give a damn if that big one there is the Emperor of the Martians or not. They're all buttholes if you ask me."

"Well, I assure you that my role as Martian Emperor is purely ceremonial," Dar said. "We really don't have an actual Martian government. But we're only along on this journey to assist with negotiating peace in Alpha Centauri."

"Yeah, yeah, yeah, ain't that nice." Rogers turned to Jack. "You there. If you people don't mind, I'd like to request that you repair the damage you've done to our ship and let us be on our way."

"And what way is that?" Jack said. "You still haven't told us."

Rogers shrugged. Nathan Pollard, sitting next to him, scrunched lower into his own chair and muttered: "No business of yours, I suppose."

"It *is* business of mine. You were sending out an SOS, and we picked you up. I'd like to know what you were doing aboard an enemy ship out here in the middle of nowhere. You evidently had a problem with your Star Drive, or you wouldn't be crawling along in the middle of nowhere at 25,000 miles an hour."

"Aaah, the AC excuse for Star Drive is worthless," Pollard said. "See, we're refugees. We stole the ship. But their Warp Transfer system is always breaking down. Most of the time it doesn't work, and it either kills everyone on board or they have to radio back for help."

"Yeah, no wonder they've never tried to mount an invasion of our solar system," Phil put in. "Most of their fleet wouldn't get there."

"They have enough trouble just getting supplies around their own set of solar systems," Will Connors said. "Of course, we're not very happy with our own Star Drive at the moment."

Dar felt Rogers' eyes on him, no doubt accessing information about the *Typhoon's* Star Drive problem. Rogers was starting to realize he didn't have to ask questions, but just get the answer from the Martians.

"So our damn Warp Transfer blew maybe an hour ago," Pollard went on. "We were stuck. We argued about sending an SOS, 'cause we knew we were dead either way. Slow death or pissed-off AC's wanting their ship back, take your pick. Finally we sent it. We couldn't figure the Centaurian code, but Bobby here knew the standard one. So *you* came. I imagine you'll have a few AC's on you within a day or two."

Jack grimaced. He'd evidently been expecting adulation, but the newcomers didn't seem at all grateful that Jack had saved them.

"So your own Star Drive's out?" Rogers said.

"Unfortunately, yes," Jack said. "We'll get it repaired at Station One. Meanwhile, we just cruise in at one-fifth light. Should be there in four months."

"Four *months?*" whimpered Sheila McCasland.

"That's how we felt at first," Joe put in. "But we really have no choice."

"Maybe you should have let us be."

"But why? You'd have drifted for eternity, or else the AC's would've caught up to you and killed you for sure."

"Maybe not. They always treated us real nice."

"Are you kidding? The Centaurians are monsters! Their policy is to kill every human they meet without question! I'd like to know how you think you could expect otherwise from them."

Sheila shrugged. "I don't know …" Dar watched her adjust her bra straps under her white blouse. She was short and had enormous breasts. She spoke in a monotone with half-closed eyes.

"What my wife means to say is that the Centaurians aren't really quite as bad as they're made out to be," McCasland put in.

"Aw, shut up," Rogers said. "These guys obviously want to believe the horror stories, so let 'em be." He looked sharply at Dar. "Hey, I just realized somethin', guys!" He pointed to Jack. "This guy here is really the head of the USSF! I can't believe it! The same jerks who started this damn war in the first place!"

Jack flushed. "Well, I *am* head of the USSF. I just didn't think you needed to know that straight off."

"But as a matter of fact, we're on a peace mission," Joe put in. "As head of the USSF, Jack has a new strategy. See, we all know the war is senseless."

"You can say that again!" Pollard hooted.

"But we're going to go in and negotiate. Isn't that right, Jack?"

"Right," Jack said. "It's a new era."

"Forget it," Rogers said. "The USSF is so hated in Alpha Centauri that you just mention you're USSF and kapow! Meson bombs everywhere!"

There was a long silence. Finally Jack said: "Well, I'm not sure I understand your story. You say you're refugees. From where?"

Rogers and Pollard exchanged a hooded look. Finally McCasland spoke up. "We were part of a settlement colony on Zorax. About a hundred fifty of us."

"Yeah, what a farce," Rogers said. "If there was one thing that really irked the AC's, it was our attempting to settle on their worlds."

"I agree it was a stupid policy," Jack said. "But that was the United System's decision, not the USSF's."

"Aw, what the hell did it matter?" Arbold Protor burst in. "The AC's hated us for it! They'll never forgive us! No wonder they wanted to wipe us out!"

"They killed our daughter Winifred," said Catherine Protor. "They were *angry*."

"Zorax is the Zarj homeworld," said Arbold, "even though the Zarj don't live there anymore. It's just an agricultural base for them. But we sinned all over that world! And we knew it would come to their vengeance upon us!"

There was another silence. Jack said: "Then why did you people volunteer for the settlement program?"

"We don't know," said McCasland. "Maybe for the money. But Arbold's right. We sinned. And we're paying the price."

"We had a hundred fifty," Pollard said. "A hundred fifty suckers. And one day the Zarj landed and said: now we're gonna fry you. They tortured all of us. They killed people right and left. They got the bright idea of using some of us as hostages, thinking to force the USSF to move all humans out of the Zorax system. But they just couldn't control themselves. They started killing the hostages just for the fun of it. Finally we saw our chance to escape and we took it. There were nine of us on that ship, and only four Zarj at the time. We gassed them with Z-gas, then shoved them into an escape craft. Ben here, and also Emory, know spaceships, and we figured how to work their Warp Transfer drive and get the ship pointed toward Sol."

"So the United System was your goal, then?" Jack said.

"Of course."

"So why were you being so evasive a while back about your intentions?"

"We don't have to reveal anything."

"Okay, have it your way." Jack paced. "You realize this puts me in an uncomfortable position. Here I am, about to meet with representatives of the Centaurian Empire, granted they agree to meet me. But now I'm harboring nine people who've stolen a Centaurian craft. I'm sure you realize the penalty for stealing a Centaurian ship is death."

"Of course we realize that," Rogers snapped. "But for them, the penalty for being a human is also death."

"Yeah, okay. The point is, I'm going to have to hide you until the negotiations are over. You'll have to live in those staterooms." Jack pointed to the series of rooms ringing the Pod.

"Forget it. Just get your finheads here to repair our ship with their--whatever they call it--their Amplified Thought, and we'll take our chances."

"Take your chances? They'll come after the ship and find you on it. Are you kidding?" Jack turned to Dar. "I just got an idea. We can slow 'em down, if you guys'll just blow that ship up. Make it look as if they had a real bad interflow cross-up on their Star Drive. They'll find the pieces and stop looking."

"Good idea, Jack," Joe said.

Rogers shrugged. "I don't care. Put us back on it first. Then when they find all the gristle and guts, they can--"

"Sir, I've had enough of your insolent attitude!" Jack flared. "We've rescued you from certain death, and you might show a little gratitude."

"Aw, cripes, man."

"And you might realize as well that since this is wartime, and since you're all aboard my ship, you'll follow my orders without question! Is that understood?"

The nine refugees looked at the floor in unconcerned exhaustion. "Joe," Jack went on, "after we repair the Augmented Nuke, we'll have Phil help the Martians visualize the AC Warp Transfer system and we'll engineer a pretty convincing disaster."

"I'll get to work on it right after we're done," Joe replied.

Carl Rogers screwed up his long, rubbery face. "Listen, I'm sorry if I've struck you as insolent, sir. But I must request that you allow us to attempt our own escape in our own way. We request that you allow us to use the Centaurian ship."

"Request denied," Jack snapped. "It's insane. You're chancing certain death. And if you'll read Dar's mind you'll understand why we can't repair your Star Drive system. We simply don't have the technical knowledge of AC systems to do it."

"Typical USSF BS," Rogers muttered.

"*What'd* you say to me, sir?"

"Aaah, piss on it."

"I will not have this insolence on my ship! Is that understood? Now, I welcome you all aboard as comrades. There's even a lot of work we can do together if you want to help our effort. I also understand you're exhausted by your ordeal, and will need some time to rest."

"Aw, cut the patronizing crap. We know you don't understand what's really going on in the Centaurian system. You're all jerks!"

Jack stood over the lounging Rogers. "Listen to me. We have four AC veterans on board today. Connors, Borman, James, and Sperry here all know firsthand about Alpha Centauri. And the rest of us have prepared for this mission for months. I can tell you the names and ascension dates of all the Centaurian Emperors two thousand years back. I don't need you telling me I don't understand the situation here!"

"I'm afraid Mr. Rogers might have a point, Jack," Patrick James cut in.

"What?" Jack cried, whirling. James stood with meekly folded hands. Was he sick? Dar wondered. "What are you saying, James? Did I ask you to butt in on this, Lieutenant?"

"Jack, I just wanted to sort of balance the argument out, you know. I really don't think you're being fair to our guests."

"I have bent over backwards to be fair to our guests!"

"I mean, being fair in the sense of putting yourself in their shoes. Of understanding where they're coming from. Of even bothering to understand the political situation in Alpha Centauri in the first place."

"I just got through saying that I did understand the situation, Lieutenant! I do not understand the reason for your insubordinate outburst!"

James stood in front of the newcomers, head lowered, and smiled. "Jack, don't you get it? Someone has to stand up for these brave souls. And it might as well be me. For I understand them."

"Patrick James understands," Nathan Pollard said. "He, at least, we can count as a friend on board this ship. He understands what we've really been through, in the deepest part of our souls."

"You see, Jack, the colonists were used badly, by both the United System Council and the USSF," James went on. "They were fed a lot of lies about how good life in the Centaurian system would be, when in reality they were just sent in as sort of dirt-cheap occupying forces. The Council hoped that humans would root there, expand to billions with the aid of fertility drugs, and prove too numerous to get rid of. And the riches of Alpha Centauri would belong to the United System, and sooner or later genocide would be the fate of any indigenous AC species."

"I'll grant the program was stupid, but that's all it was-- stupid," Jack said. "Nobody was smart enough to plan a United System takeover of Alpha Centauri."

"Oh, but that's where you're mistaken. The United System Council lusted after pure power! And so did our goody-two-shoes USSF! Power and domination! Fresh worlds to plunder! The beginnings of a galactic empire!"

"He's right, Commer," Rogers said. "I might add that we colonists were considered expendable. The more of us slaughtered by the AC's, the better it would look in the media back home, and the more support for genocide on the Centaurians."

"I can't believe this!" Amav put in. "These monsters killed

your loved ones, and you're taking their side?"

"Yes, in a way we do take their side," Rogers said. "They've suffered terribly at our hands, and their response is, I think, quite justified."

"Are you crazy? Torture and killing? Of children? Of noncombatants? My God, nothing justifies that!"

"Talk to your comrade James," Pollard said. "*He* understands."

"Look, just can the political theorizing for now," Jack said. "We all need some rest. We've got a lot of stuff to do. Like take care of the AC ship, for one thing."

"I must repeat my demand that you repair our ship and let us be on our way," Rogers said.

"No! And James, you sit down this instant!" To Dar's shock James was stroking Anna Dorch's long gray hair.

"I'm sorry, Jack," James said. "But I have a higher duty right now, to soothe my comrades here."

Jack stared, speechless. Dar found himself on his feet, realizing what was making him uneasy. The same thing that was so disturbing about the newcomers was also in James. James had the same glazed look as the newcomers.

"You--you--" Jack sputtered. "You fools! Don't you understand this is what the Centaurians *want* you to think? That *they're* the oppressed ones, that they're peace-loving and gentle and that the USSF messed it up entirely on its own? Hell, I know we've made mistakes in the past, but I also know that it's the Centaurians' insane aggressiveness that's kept the war going! They're totally irrational! The last time we contacted their Emperor with an offer to pull out all military forces and establish trade, they demanded that the entire human race commit suicide to the last person! Now does that make sense? They threatened to invade Mars and torture everything they could get their hands on, from humans down to cats and dogs! Is that rational?"

"This is simply a typical USSF response to a complex situation," Rogers said. "You simply don't understand how the USSF has manipulated the Centaurians into making all those statements, which are purely for internal consumption. The

Emperor, in order to achieve lasting peace, has to maintain a semblance of military show for his advisors and the Imperial Assembly."

"And the Centaurians don't seriously *torture,*" Pollard put in. "That's all USSF lies."

"We know," James said. "These damn USSF'ers all know it, but won't admit it."

"I can't believe you said that!" Jack said. He pointed to Pollard. "And this guy just got through saying that the Zarj tortured and killed all but the nine from his colony!"

"We knew it was self-defense on their part," Pollard said.

"It's like cleaning up garbage," said Anna Dorch. "Or killing roaches. We're like roaches to them."

"So you're justifying the Centaurians killing your family and friends?" Jack cried.

"Yes."

The silence went on so long that Dar sincerely wished to die rather than endure it. Anna went on: "Our plan is to journey to Sol and spread the *truth* about the Centaurians. Then we want to return to Zorax and live in harmony with our Centaurian brethren."

"You can't be serious!" Jack said.

"They *are* serious," James said.

"I thought I told you to sit down and shut up, Lieutenant!"

"No, Jack. Not this time. I'm through with all this USSF bull."

Instantly Jack had his shattergun out and trained on James' chest. "James, this is the second time today I've had to pull a shattergun on a crewmember. I'm in no mood for jokes. You are to sit down and shut up as of this second. You will receive a more detailed reprimand later."

"Forget it!" James pulled his USSF I.D. card off his shirt pocket and with some difficulty ripped the plastic tag in half and threw the pieces to the floor. "I quit the USSF, Commer! I'm joining my friends here! We'll spread the *truth* about the Centaurians!" He ripped at the insignia on his shoulders but only succeeded in tearing his left sleeve off.

"Lieutenant James, you're under arrest. You're relieved of all duties and will be confined to Stateroom One for the duration of this voyage. If you do not immediately surrender yourself, and this includes shutting up entirely, I will shatter you instantly. You may give your acknowledgment by nodding your head."

James shrugged, smirked, and finally nodded. Joe clamped force field handcuffs behind James' back, herded him to Stateroom One and pushed him so hard that he stumbled headlong into a wall. Joe kicked James' feet fully inside and locked the door.

"We can't have that," was his comment when he returned to the group.

"My, you sure know how to enforce discipline here," Rogers said.

"Rogers, you stay shut up yourself," Jack said. "You leave my crew alone."

Rogers smiled. "So you begin to suspect the truth, eh?"

"I'm not sure I know what you mean by that, but if you had anything to do with James' little fit back there, I'll blow you all away without a second thought. As a matter of fact, I think I'll confine all of you to Staterooms Two through Ten immediately. Joe, prepare the staterooms for all nine of our guests."

"Death to the USSF!" came a muffled shriek from Stateroom One. "Long live the Centaurians!"

"Jack," Dar said, "there was something about James' *eyes*. All these people have it, too. The *eyes*."

"What do you mean?"

"I'm not sure. It's just that I've gotten used to how you humans look, your facial expressions, and something's wrong here, with all of them."

"Except the boy," Amav put in. "I know what you mean, Dar. But not the boy. You there--Bobby?"

The twelve-year-old raised his head. "Yes, ma'am?"

"Look at me." Amav looked into Bobby's eyes. "Tell me, Bobby, are the Centaurians your friends?"

"No, ma'am. They killed my Mom and Dad."

"Bobby, they had to," Anna Dorch cut in. "They were

teaching you a lesson."

Bobby gazed dully at her.

"Bobby, do you want to kill those AC's? The ones who killed your parents?" Amav asked. Bobby didn't reply. "Do you want to kill them?"

Finally Bobby shook his head. "No. I just want to be left alone."

"The kid's obviously too disoriented by the whole thing to know right from wrong," Rogers said. "But he'll find out that the Centaurians can be understood, and lived with. It'll all work out."

"You know, Jack," Lee Borman said, "these guys may have some sort of point after all. I mean, this is why we're going to Alpha Centauri in the first place, right? To negotiate, to understand the enemy. And hopefully make him into a friend. Smooth out all the misunderstandings. I mean, look, Jack, let's be a little more understanding of our guests. After all, they have some firsthand experience we don't." Once more Borman stared down the barrel of Jack's shattergun.

"His *eyes,*" Joe whispered.

"Borman," Jack said, "are you a loyal member of this crew or not?"

Borman eyed the gun. "Uh, s-sure, Jack. You know I am."

"All right, then. Cut the traitor talk and help Joe lock our guests up. All except Bobby there. He'll first report to Sperry for a medical checkup and then to me for a little discussion."

Dar watched in relief as the other eight refugees were locked into the staterooms.

CHAPTER EIGHT
Jack's Diary
Friday, March 16, 2035, 2100 hours

Tonight I got so angry I decided to stop the stupid diary-keeping once and for all. Spent an hour getting so angry, so out of control, that I really thought, this is it, I'm beginning to cave in after all. To the Head. Whatever that is.

Then I thought: no, I'm stronger than that. It may take a few more weeks, and the depressions just keep getting worse until I can't bear it any longer, but I've made up my mind to withstand it to the end. God, it's crazy that it's come to this.

Sperry went just yesterday. His diary entry was shocking. Totally insane. And it was his idea to use diary-keeping in the first place. I thought he was solid. That's one reason I've been so depressed all day. Just sitting here, locked in the Control Room as usual. Didn't even get up to use the bathroom until 2000 hours.

I guess Sperry was right. Having everyone keep diaries was a good way of pinpointing when someone's mind finally broke down. When the *conversion* hit. It's been weird, reading the diaries of the three Martians, Joe, and Sperry, and then suddenly seeing the brainwashing kick in. In most cases the break was pretty dramatic. Suddenly the writing launched into praises of the Head and the Emperor. Sometimes there'd follow a day or two of further entries, crazier and crazier until they finally stopped. Borman and Connors sparked all this when they converted the first week. Now, counting James, who'd defected the very first day, three of my crew were gone. I knew there was a problem. Something was getting into our minds. Sperry suggested the diaries, and I ordered everyone to submit them by email.

Can't begin to think about Joe. Haven't been thinking of him. He converted nine days ago. I would've assumed he'd have been with us to the end. Well, I guess I assumed that about Sperry, too. Guess I assume it about myself. And Amav and Bobby. That we'll never convert. Certain things I can't write

69

about, though. Maybe in a way we've already converted and just don't know it.

The only reason I'm writing now is that I got so angry back there. I see I've been doing my diary just like everyone else all these weeks, holding back, writing mechanical little reports of what we've been doing, but never really coming out and saying anything. As if we've all been afraid to show any real emotion, as if that's the first step to conversion. Well, the diaries never could show who was about to convert, only who'd just converted. From Sperry's view of preventive medicine, it's been a silly failure.

Yeah, I've been covering up all this time. But now I know I have to get everything out. I can't believe I'm putting all this down so directly. I've never done it before, and it feels weird. I guess I'm thinking in the back of my mind that if the USSF captures this ship someday, probably after destroying all of us on board to quarantine this disease, I want them to have a real record of what's been going on.

My ship's log won't show it. It's even drier than my diary entries. I've never liked writing stuff down. I feel like I'm baring my soul to strangers. But I have to tell the whole story of what happened since we picked up the refugees. Because I really don't know how long I'll last. I'm sitting here at my command station typing as fast as I can. Don't know why I still use the keyboard. Maybe I'm being superstitious. The people who survived the longest have been the ones using the keyboard and actually writing: me, Joe, Sperry, Amav, even Bobby. At first I wanted to allow voice recordings, but Sperry wondered if "just talking" wasn't good enough, that maybe actual writing would keep us focused. So I ordered all diaries submitted as keyboarded documents. But now I see what illusory comfort that was.

The Martians gave me the weirdest diaries of all. Of course I could read their minds whenever I wanted to, and I can read them right now, but it's so trivial and chaotic it makes me nauseous. But even the Martians knew it would take a long time to sift through all those thoughts to get an accurate picture of where they stood psychologically. So Dar proposed that the Martians create within each of their minds a special file where they'd dump selected thoughts to make up a coherent diary. Then all I had to do at the end of each day was access that special file. Very neat, and their diaries were complete in every respect. The only thing wrong was that the Martians were the next to convert after Borman and Connors. None of us could believe it. Noble Martians, thousands of years old! And they all converted simultaneously.

It was then that we knew we were in serious danger, and I decided, although I'd previously locked all converted personnel in the Pod staterooms, that none of the rest of us could ever go in the Pod again. I had to free the prisoners from the staterooms so they could access food and other necessities from the Pod's stores. So of the nineteen beings under my care now, sixteen are locked under us in the Pod: eight refugees, three Martians, and five of my crewmen including my brother, apparently all having the time of their lives cavorting around in the .38 gravity and having philosophical discussions about "the Head" and their duty to the Emperor of the Alpha Centaurians.

But within a few days I'd made an exception for Bobby. I've found that he can report objectively to me what's going on down there. And I need to know. Tuning into the Martians sure doesn't hack it. Their thoughts are like browsing through a million Mother's Day card racks in search of some nugget of useful data that's just never going to be there. Sometimes their doped-up, cliché-ridden thoughts creep into my head during the day like tinny elevator music. It's disgusting.

But for some crazy reason Bobby seems invulnerable to this Head business, maybe because he's so damn imploded, and I thought, even if he does convert, it's no big loss to my ship's functioning. I admit this is a bit callous, but I have to know what's going on down there. Have to know if there's any chance I can ever get Joe back, or if I'm going to have to jettison the Pod and kill everyone over there.

I gave Bobby the title of "ambassador" between the ship and the Pod. I'd hoped it would raise his morale, but it's apparently had little effect. I admit he does go about his job with zeal. And hell, bravery. Because the only way I can allow him in there is to lock him in for a while, and he knows it. The ventral hatch between the *Typhoon* and the Pod is protected by a code lock. I've given Bobby the code to open it from our side, but to get back, he has to call me on the intercom and ask me to let him back inside. Only Bobby and I know the code to get into the Pod, but only I know the code to get back to the *Typhoon* from the Pod. Of course I had to change all the codes when we threw Sperry in there last night.

I've also let everyone on board know that the ventral hatch is ringed with blasters set to incinerate anyone who attempts to tamper with the code lock.

This Head business. So far all I can find out about it, and this despite the fact that I can read Dar's thoughts this second and still understand nothing out of that chaos, is that it's sort of like the mind reading we do off the Martians, except that the "mind" you're supposed to be able to read *isn't there*. God knows where or what it is. All the Converted (as they refer to themselves in obvious uppercase) can do is froth on and on about the Head and the Emperor and how wonderful the Centaurians are. They say they're in constant contact with this Head, and it seems to be a source of great comfort to them all. I can see how the Martians got sucked in by their curiosity. Apparently Rogers was describing the Head to them as being like reading a human being's mind, and the Martians had to be curious about that.

I have to admit it: I'm really scared now. This whole mission is a disaster. I can't even begin to consider how my being here, facing conversion and death, cut off from USSF Command for a month and a half now, is affecting the entire political situation. I know I've never given enough thought to my status as Supreme Commander of the USSF, with more power than even Blerthen, head of the United System Council. I've tried to pretend I'm still a jock test pilot, that being USSF Commander is just a big cash bonus for being a good boy. Well, I've messed it up. Probably Bob Easterling has assumed command now. What a worthless jerk. I should never have left him in charge of headquarters while I was gone. But he has no choice but to assume command, and I imagine he did it shortly after our loss of contact. Although right now I don't see any clear alternative to ending the Centaurian War other than by black-holing every sun in their empire, still I came here to attempt otherwise, and I know Easterling won't even try any alternatives. Worse yet, he'll try to do the black-holing with ships nowhere near the *Typhoon* class, and probably at such a slow rate that the Centaurians will see how it's done, and send a few ships back to Sol to practice the technique on *our* sun. Their scientists aren't stupid; they black-holed Barnard's Star themselves last year, though they lost a major ship in the bargain. But now they can measure and observe the *Doomboat*-class battle cruisers as they take up orbits around their suns, and figure out how to do the deed without loss to themselves.

Can't believe I've screwed up this badly. Can't believe I placed the fate of humanity in the balance here, and failed. In a few days I'll be brainwashed into being one of *them,* I'll be their tool. We'd heard rumors of this Head business before we set out, we knew the AC's were a hive mentality, but did we really prepare for encountering that? No way! We just thought we could waltz in with the most powerful spaceship in existence and dictate some sort of cosmic friendship to these monsters. And to see everyone sucked into this, the refugees, my crew, the Martians, and Joe! I can't believe anyone would buy into this Head crap, this worship of the Centaurian Emperor.

And all I can do is think back to Huey Vespertine's goddamn interview with us before we left, and his cackling predictions of failure and doom. And he was right. That bastard always has some wiseass, cynical way of twisting things around to him always being right! I completely turned my back on him when he dropped out of the Academy. I didn't care that we'd been friends his first and only year there. I know Joe's maintained some contact and I've always tried to ignore that. Joe always says I must be secretly fascinated with Huey's eccentricities and his irreverent attitude towards everything, but that crap he's always spouting about the USSF being a militarist tool of empire has always turned my stomach. That fat blob is a damn traitor to humanity.

But he predicted our failure! Perfectly!

But you know, and it's totally crazy, I really just can't concentrate on any of that. It's just too immense. I just can't picture the loss of our whole solar system, or anybody else's, once you get down to it. And here I am, thirty-one years old and I have the power to wipe out stars.

Or did have the power. Without Star Drive, I can't do it. Without superspace radio I sure can't order *Doomboat* battle cruisers to do it for me. It's strange, but I'm just now realizing that the whole game is out of my hands. Maybe it just has to be pure survival on my part now. Mental survival. Maybe somehow writing all this down is part of that process. Can I possibly hold out until we get to Station One?

Am I kidding myself? I've witnessed people I thought totally sane succumb to conversion. Borman and Connors and the Martians. Maybe I could understand them converting, even turning traitor to Sol. But *Joe*--to this day I can't believe it. I'd really thought we were down to a stable unit of me, Amav, Joe, and Sperry. But on March 7th, a week and a half ago, Joe was sitting right next to me here, and suddenly went into an incredible coughing fit. When he looked up, he had the *eyes*. The vacant, yet somehow charged-up *eyes*. And he said: "Jack, we've been wrong all along! We've been trampling on the rights of the Centaurians!"

I had to get so cold, I had to get my shattergun out and hold it on my own brother! Sperry and I had to take him down and throw him into the Pod. I was in shock. Amav's little message at the end of her diary entry didn't help either, where she talked about knowing how close Joe and I were, that of course there would be a solution, blah-blah-blah. I blasted back a short reply that put her in her place. What could she possibly know about how close Joe and I were?

So Joe's in the Pod now, with all its comfort and luscious food supplies intended for official receptions with the Centaurians, and all its recreational facilities. All that's being used by those morons down there. I'd jettison the Pod this instant if it weren't for Joe. Somehow I can't be angry at my own brother. If anyone can be deconverted, wouldn't it have to be Joe? I just don't know. I guess the *Typhoon I* always pulled us together in some mystical way. Then we lost the crew. We lost our two brothers! We were the last survivors. We always wondered why we weren't on board the *Typhoon I* when it went down. Now I'm the last survivor. Joe's gone. And I wonder why *I* haven't converted.

Then, just last night--Sperry. Somehow, even after Joe, I was certain Phil would never crack. But I locked him in the Pod at gunpoint last night after reading his diary entry. He didn't resist. There was some stuff in there about Amav that sickened me. He's promised me one more entry, not that I care to get it. Why should I want to read AC propaganda and insanity? He even hinted that he'd like to convert me with it. But that won't happen. I'm still too strong. I know how idiotic that propaganda is. I can read the Martians and see it. Fulr is particularly obnoxious on that score. But I always think: I wonder how I'll look, spouting out that same propaganda when the USSF finally boards this vessel? When we're in close enough radio range, I'll send a message telling them to destroy this ship before they get infected.

Is there really an infection? I don't know. I just don't know why the human mind suddenly collapses and starts in on this Head business. I don't know what it all means. Sperry had some interesting ideas on the subject. I know he's had some psychological training. But I'm so angry at him I can't think straight.

I should have picked up this infection angle from the beginning. Even when Phil and I were herding the refugees out of the Zarj cruiser, I could tell. I could see it in their eyes even then. Totally gone. And it seems permanent. Brain burned out, or something. Sperry wanted to kill one of the refugees and do an autopsy. I wish I'd let him. I'd like to perform several autopsies on the loyal legions of the Head right now.

From reading Martian minds, we found that the real purpose

of the refugees was to infect the United System with defeatism. They may have stolen a Zarj ship, but what they wanted to use it for was to spread their nasty little colony of Head to Sol. Only the fact that their own Star Drive malfunctioned prevented them from cruising on into Sol and starting the infection there.

In any case, I have to recognize that with Sperry gone, the last hope that this mission can succeed is also gone. Although he repaired the Augmented Nuke sublight drive with the Martians' help within a few days of our accident, and we'd easily established a maximum cruising speed of one-fifth light for our four-month journey to Alpha Centauri, it was basically a jury-rigged repair and it's going to be difficult and perhaps impossible to slow us down once we get to Alpha Centauri. Since we haven't been near a sun all this time, our solar rechargers haven't been working to replenish the Augmented Nuke for a normal deceleration, and I need Phil monitoring and retuning the engine. And though the reactor drive is shut down as we coast, driving it up to one-fifth light was a huge strain in the first place, and Sperry was supposed to have checked it out in a couple days. I'm not even sure it'll be safe to apply deceleration drive now.

I also don't have a navigator. I need to stop at Station One and get our Star Drive repaired, but it may take days of maneuvering to get there. And when I finally get there, I may find it blown to pieces. I may find myself in a combat situation with several dozen AC warships. I have some PlanetBlaster functionality, but it's damn limited right now.

I'm alone. Sure, Amav's back there, sitting in Borman's old turret, as far away from me as she can get. She sure doesn't understand the reactor, or anything else that happens on this ship.

Well, I can see I'm still avoiding the main subject. It obviously has a place here. Since I swore to be honest, I guess I have to come out and say it: the main reason this mission has failed is that Amav and I aren't speaking to each other. We haven't spoken since the day the Martians converted. That was Friday, February 16. One month ago! We were arguing about who really lost the Martians or some such nonsense. I can't even remember what we were talking about. It was totally insane, it went on for an hour, everyone else just tried to ignore it. She was screaming that if the Martians went, we were doomed, and I threatened to jail her for treason! Can you believe that? One month of absolutely no talking. It's over. The marriage fell completely apart.

I don't know why. Or maybe I do know why and can't say it. I don't even know how I feel about it. It's been absolutely crazy, having ordered everyone to give me diary entries, including my own wife, and getting these dry little weather reports.

"Felt secure in the morning. Thought about the Centaurians in the afternoon. Spent several hours studying the stars from the dorsal turret tonight." Little four-sentence entries when of course I want to know more. I admit it: I've been wishing she'd use the diary to start talking to me. To say something real. I probably messed up when I shot back my nasty reply after her diary entry about Joe. I don't know. I was hoping she'd argue back with me. But she sure didn't care enough to.

That was why I was so angry tonight. This whole diary fiasco started as a need to chronicle my crewmembers' mental states, but everyone's been completely dishonest. Even Bobby, our last remaining sane person besides Amav and myself. All he's done is write obnoxious little science fiction stories. He's obsessed with old wars, especially the American Civil War, and finally this afternoon I screamed at him, no more Civil War stories! Amav saw me do this and turned away in disgust. It's the only time I've seen her in a week. Meanwhile Bobby just shrugged. He's a zombie.

What's even weirder is that it struck me at that moment that Bobby represented our child. This totally uncommunicative, obsessed, warped kid, but nevertheless somehow unbrainwashed by the Head. What a family we make! Amav and I on opposite ends of the ship, Bobby passing freely back and forth between the realms of mental illness and the so-called sanity aboard the *Typhoon*.

This is the first time I've written anything like this down. In fact, it's the first time I've really even thought about it. It's the first time I've written down that I've exiled myself to the Control Room since Joe converted. I was so upset by that, and so angry at Amav, so needing to be away from her, that I've simply been shut up in this room for a week and a half. I go to the bathroom midships a couple times a day, maybe the kitchenette a couple times, but I now store most of my food in the Control Room. Sperry noticed it before he converted, but never said a word.

And ever since I found out last night about all of Sperry's fantasies about her, I've been wondering. What was going on down at the other end of the ship? Was she screwing him? Well, maybe it doesn't matter at this point. All I know, and the madder I get as I write this, is that--well, I'm getting incoherent. I can't kill Sperry. I can't kill anyone. I'm so sick of all this insanity. I don't want to hurt anyone. Not Amav, not anyone.

I'll never know if they were lovers. I guess I'll just sit in here until either the AC's or the USSF find us. If the AC's find us, I'll put up a fight, fire the PlanetBlasters by remote control, enough to rile them up, then maybe they'll destroy the ship. Maybe I should do that with the USSF as well: act hostile, maybe they'll destroy us that way.

Sometimes she sits in the radar room. But mostly in the turret. God, I couldn't stand it, just staring at the stars for hours on end. I've drawn the steel shutters over the Control Room windows because I can't stand the stars. I can hear her use the bathroom now and then. We seem to have evolved this weird schedule of when we're each going to use the bathroom. For instance, I know she'd never be there at 2000 hours, when I was last there. I could always tell if it was Joe or Sperry or Bobby using the bathroom, because they didn't take as long in there. And usually Joe or Sperry would check in with me anyway. I began talking to them, when they were still sane, that is, hoping Amav would hear and be drawn into the conversation. Somehow.

I can't approach her. Isn't that unbelievable? This is my wife, after all. I still admire her, I guess. Have to, she's held out as long as I have, as long as Bobby has. The final survivors. What terrible irony. Or maybe we're just holding out because we're both so stubborn. We don't like to change our ways, we're so argumentative, we won't give on anything. We're just refusing to convert out of pure orneriness. Maybe we're both just psychological misfits, too screwed up to undergo what Sperry called in his diary last night "the final bliss of dissolution." We have too many ego problems to allow ourselves to flow with that drugged bliss. Maybe I'm almost ready for it myself. The Martians sometimes call to me. I always reject it. Amav must too. We just hold on here. God, would I love to hold her in my arms again, start taking her clothes off! Wouldn't that be wonderful? Wouldn't that solve everything?

But *divorce* is in the way, *divorce* destroys that. We're permanently apart. You can see it in her eyes. It's pure contempt for me that's kept her diary on the level of inane fluff. She's tormenting me and knows it. And I've wasted a month and a half writing tidy little diary entries when all along I could have been writing like I am now. Getting this insanity out into the open. Where I suppose it belongs.

God, to write this down confirms it all. I've been a mess, and I've ruined this mission and all of our lives. Amav tried to crack my rigid identity and all my games, and maybe she succeeded. But instead of cracking me open to free me from a prison, she cracked open my life support systems and now my air is gone, my pressure is gone. She's finished me. My games and her games have collided and exploded.

The proof of this is the fact that even in this moment of crisis, even in this life-and-death situation, neither of us will try to cooperate to ensure our survival. We don't *want* to survive.

God, is this how you convert? Is this how you feel when you give up? Is it even possible to struggle against this?

CHAPTER NINE
Amav's Diary
Friday, March 16, 2035, 2100 hours

I can't continue with this farce of diary-keeping any longer. When Jack herded Phil into the Pod at gunpoint last night, I knew our stupid game was finally up. Although Bobby may somehow be immune to conversion, I now realize nobody else is. It's down to Jack and me. And we're both going to go soon and right now I don't care. I've decided I'm going to commit suicide rather than let my brain get warped like that. Maybe it has to be tonight, before I'm converted. I can feel it coming. I'm so tired.

And Jack isn't going to read this. This is my last diary entry but I'm not going to send it to the Control Room. Being honest here is something I need for myself, and I'm sick of hiding myself in sterile diary entries.

I've been scared. I can admit that. I've been scared and I haven't wanted to know it. Scared that if I started voicing things openly, I might somehow contribute to converting others. Both James and Borman suddenly started expressing deeper parts of themselves, just before their eyes went blank with the full force of the conversion. They both became incredibly animated and open, their souls pouring right out of their eyes, their hands, the tone of their voices. So I've been careful to keep things buttoned up.

But the main reason I've withheld myself is that I was damned if I was going to let Jack know what's been going on. He's always demanded a printout of my mind anyway. This whole diary-keeping project has been his way of keeping tabs on me. I knew he'd analyze my entries and dissect them and tell me what was wrong with me. Besides, Jack has been so full of hatred for me, for himself, for everyone, that I could see the arguments, the shrieking, that would follow one straightforward diary entry.

I'm writing this now because I want whoever finds this ship someday to know the reasons why our mission failed. Some sort of truthful record needs to be kept. But of course Jack will never see it.

It's horrible to realize that Jack has snapped. The stress of this entire mission has wiped him out, all the months of preparation, his getting the USSF command, and this current fiasco. My own husband. He's gone. I can't believe it. I guess I've been trying for months to ignore this. It's been even more bitter to realize that it wasn't ever a marriage. It's been unreal from the start. All sorts of romance and good times, but it caved in immediately after we were married. I didn't want to believe that.

I'm only twenty-two. I can't believe I volunteered for this mission. I can't believe it was me who suggested bringing the Martians along and turning the mission towards fact-finding and peace. But I may have screwed it up by my presence. Something's turned Jack inside out. He's been so irritated at me. It has to be me.

But that's stupid! If he can't work with me, he should've realized it and stopped the whole thing at the beginning. Instead he just allowed it to get more and more screwed up. Sometimes I think this whole conversion stuff pales in comparison.

We haven't spoken since the day the Martians converted a month ago. And he was the one who stormed away and screamed he never wanted to see me again! I just stood there with my mouth open. How were we to function, how were we to fight this conversion menace, if we didn't see each other? The answer, as I later found, was that we *weren't* supposed to fight together. I was cut out of all ship routines by Jack's order. Joe and Phil, when they were still sane, were ordered not to speak to me, although both did. I was exiled to Borman's turret, and I just sat there all day reading novels from the ship's library on my computer.

Jack thought that locking everyone who'd converted in the Pod and keeping the "sane ones" on the *Typhoon* would quarantine the disease, and then he and Joe and Phil could bring the ship to Station One. He didn't count on me being the last person left except for Bobby.

Right after Joe converted, I sent Jack a message. I would have said it in person, but I knew he'd explode. So I included it at the end of my diary entry. It was the one attempt I've made to be honest. Pasting this in from my 3/7 diary:

"Jack, look, I've been thinking. We need to fight this thing together. Believe me, I know how close you are to your brother. I know what you must be feeling. But with Joe gone, you need me as a functioning crew member. Let's forget whatever's wrong between us, and, for the good of the ship, for the mission, let's cooperate, beat this danger, and find some way to get Joe and the others back."

And Jack's reply, received at three in the morning? And I also dump this out of my files. I saved it knowing it was the last piece of communication I'll ever receive from my husband:

YOU WILL NOT ATTEMPT TO MANIPULATE EMOTIONS. OTHERWISE I WILL CONFINE YOU TO POD. YOUR SCHEMING ENDANGERS ENTIRE MISSION. COMMER.

Confine me to the Pod! Put me in there with those monsters! Rogers and Pollard would rape me in a second, and Jack knows that. He also knows I'd be converted immediately. I don't think he'd do it. I think he was just trying to impress me with his little boy suffering. But for the first time I wasn't sure. I knew Jack was off his rocker. I resolved to steer clear of him.

Isn't it obvious Jack is just letting this ship drift to its doom? He doesn't give a damn whether we're all killed or not. He *wants* to submit to conversion, he *wants* the AC's to infect the United System with the Head! But I'm not supposed to say a word. So, like a coward, I sit here and wait.

I'm almost ready to put my shattergun to my head right now. The gun I refused to surrender to Jack a month ago, in fact, the gun that sparked the big fight. Despite the fact that we spent most of the fight arguing about who let the Martians get converted, as if somehow I'd caused it by being so open with my emotions, I now see it was really about the damn shattergun all along. In the middle of the fight Jack decides to lock all the Converted into the Pod, then says he's going to collect all the weapons on the ship. But he's enraged at the idea of his own wife wanting to protect herself with her own shattergun! I argued I needed it to defend myself in case the Converted broke out of the Pod, but Jack stood there sputtering with rage and jabbering about "coddling the Empress" and "the damn Empress shattergun." It was when Joe and Phil both backed me up that Jack stomped away, yelling he'd never speak to me again.

Okay, so it's the official Martian Empress cryogenic shattergun, and so Hergs did give it to me. Jack must have some sort of hang-up on this gun. Maybe it reminds him I was being conditioned into being Hergs' Empress. Of course, Jack conveniently forgets I saved his damn life with it, that I was the one who did away with Sam Hergs! Doesn't he realize that's *why* I've kept this stupid gun?

So should I end it all now? I've been feeling more and more insane, cooped up on this miserable ship, eating junk food out of the kitchenette, having no real privacy, for weeks on end. And seeing my own husband walk away from me like this.

I would never have suspected Jack is so emotionally crippled. I had boyfriends at the university, I knew my way around. Hell, by the time I'd met Jack I had six months of the Martian Erotic Teachings! I was certain I could intuit a man's basic nature fairly accurately.

Behind Jack's shy and touchingly inexperienced ways, I thought I saw an honest and romantic man, one who could care deeply about me in the deepest sense of friends and lovers. We'd be allies, we'd explore and conquer the universe together. I have to admit I proposed the new twist on the Alpha Centaurian mission because I was intoxicated with this vision of Jack and myself battling unknown evils side by side. I was sure we could win against anything.

So imagine my horror when I discovered I was married to a moody child who fears and hates me, who sees me as the major malevolence of his life. Imagine what it's like to discover that the gentle, understanding Jack Commer can threaten to leave his wife to be raped and brainwashed by mutant slime like Rogers and Pollard! Imagine what it's like to be imprisoned on this ship, waiting to die and knowing your husband fears you so much that he can't even bring himself to utter a word to you or meet your eye!

This afternoon I was particularly disgusted to come upon Jack in the fuselage, right next to the smashed escape ship we've never thought to jettison into space, berating Bobby with angry obscenities that most men would hesitate to use against someone their own age. The occasion? Bobby wrote another story with a Civil War twist, and Jack went to pieces. I was just coming out of the kitchenette when I saw Jack collar Bobby, who stood frozen through the screaming and then shrugged and walked away. Much more of a man than our madman SCUSSF.

It's sad to see Bobby facing death as well. All emotion is *gone* from the boy. I know he hasn't converted. He shows me all the stories he writes before he hands them over to Jack, and I can see him getting some of his fears and obsessions out in them. And despite his emotional flatness, Bobby and I have become good friends. We'll sit in the Sensor Room for hours, sometimes just reading novels side by side at two of the computer screens, or I'll read one of his stories and we'll talk about it for a while. Wouldn't Jack be sick to discover I've read every one of Bobby's "for Captain's eyes only" diary entries? And somehow Bobby doesn't treat me as a mother, even though you might expect him to.

I'm really just a sort of smartass older sister to him, and he's really just a smartass younger brother to me. Maybe our rapport has something to do with the fact that I'm just barely out of adolescence. How painful to admit that! And what am I doing married in the first place at this age? Twenty-two is too young! I've just left the Crazy Zone, and Bobby's just entering it. We have something in common. We have a great time together.

Which is probably one reason Jack hates Bobby. Obviously he senses that Bobby and I are friends and wants to destroy that. God, he can be so evil! I sometimes even think that he lets Bobby come and go between the two ships because he *wants* Bobby to be converted, and then he'd have an excuse to lock him away down there. I'm convinced that somehow, maybe because of his age, Bobby can't be converted. All the same, I don't want to risk it, and I even wrote in one of my diary entries my recommendation that Bobby be denied access to the Pod. This time, not a word of response from Jack. He doesn't care if a fellow human gets his or her brain completely destroyed if that should suit his petty mental disorders.

I don't know how Bobby feels about being able to go back and forth at will. He seems to take it for granted that he should be able to do so. The only hint I've found of this was in one of his stories, in which a Rebel soldier swims back and forth across a river in Kentucky, donning a Union uniform he keeps stashed in a tree and depositing his Rebel uniform there. While in the Union camp, he's known as Jake and plays cards all night long. While in the Rebel camp his name is Jonathan and he helps dig earthworks for the coming Union attack. When the attack finally comes, it's revealed that Jake/Jonathan is really a British observer, formerly an actor in London, who doesn't really understand what he's doing in the Civil War, which side he should fight on, or if he should try to escape. Although written in extremely twelve-year-old language ("And then three cannon balls spread his guts all over the place!") this particular story reverberated with adolescent despair.

The story that set Jack off yesterday had a new twist. Bobby had gotten the word to can the Civil War stories, but he wasn't about to entirely knuckle under. In this story, "Harry Patterson, Public Menace No. 1," a U.S. Air Force pilot flying an F-104 Starfighter out of Munich in 1966 (I have no idea where Bobby gets all this research) goes through a time warp and discovers that he's flying above a Civil War battlefield. For some reason, not very clear, the pilot, Harry Patterson, "goes bad," and Chapter One, "Civil War Blow-Up," ends with Patterson dropping a hydrogen bomb into the middle of the battlefield, decisively ending the combat. In subsequent scenes Patterson flies through time to 2040, where U.S. prosecutors are waiting to charge him with the murder of 10,000 soldiers during the Civil War. Patterson flees, ending up drinking a potion that makes him a giant, stomping cities, stealing a (very large) spaceship and flying to the moon to wreck an army base there. In the end Patterson dies on the moon from lack of air.

I don't know, is Bobby a little Jack? Will he grow up crazy like Jack? Will he let these problems fester until they take him over? In a way Jack's already been converted by a brainwashing that came totally from within. He's sat on his problems all his life, through adolescence and manhood, and never admitted he had them or tried to do anything about them. I only hope Bobby doesn't end up like that.

But who am I kidding? Bobby doesn't have two weeks left. None of us do. Because when Jack finally converts, whether before or after me doesn't matter, he's simply going to remove the barriers preventing access to the Pod, and Bobby is going to find himself alone amid a sea of Converted slime. And I'm sure they won't hesitate to kill him once they see he can't be converted. I won't be there to participate. I'll be a pile of shattered glass before that happens. I absolutely refuse to be part of that. I bet Jack hasn't even thought that Bobby has to die because of the conversions of the rest of us. Of course not. He can't think anything through.

For instance, isn't it obvious Jack can't manage the ship on his own? I know enough about the functioning of this ship that he can't do it without at least Phil. Phil told me that yesterday afternoon before he converted. And there's no hope of continuing the original plan of negotiating with the AC's. We would've had to go into that from a position of strength, namely, a fully functional *Typhoon II*. We'd have to be able to back up our negotiating positions with force in case things fell through.

Sure, we all hoped for some sort of understanding with the AC's, but I think we've all known from the beginning that the Centaurians respect only military force. When Admiral Cromwell brought the first fleet of USSF battle cruisers out of Star Drive in the vicinity of Alpha Centauri A, the capital star of the seventeen suns of the AC empire, the Centaurians immediately set off thousands of meson bombs around the armada as a warning. Cromwell's orders from General Scott were to get home immediately if his ships encountered any form of hostility. After all, the Articles of Exploration, developed when Star Drive was invented, state that Earth only wants to explore, not get involved in disputes with any intelligent beings we might find.

But Cromwell got macho and began attacking not only the bomb-launching ships, but also a cluster of residential spaceships far from the scene. I've always wondered if it wasn't the jangling nature of Star Drive itself that had Cromwell and his senior officers so agitated that they started firing Xon bombs. Nobody has ever been able to figure out why Cromwell so blithely committed us to interstellar war.

Was it just because we were so damn immature, so new to this space business? After all, just twenty years ago we were mothballing ancient space shuttles, we had no serious plans for manned spaceflight, we'd given up on space. And then all of a sudden all these breakthroughs, all this new technology. Superfast spaceships and heat blasters and Electron Oblivion Sequencing guns and Star Drive! Where the hell did all *that* come from? We weren't ready to handle any of it, I think everyone knew that deep down. Sure, the asteroids going into the sun in '28 scared us, and then Pluto, and the Neptune and Uranus disasters, and later on Jupiter and Saturn exploding. We were paranoid, we'd do anything to figure out what the hell was going on, and suddenly by '30 we wind up with the Xon bomb, Star Drive, and a fleet of killer battleships.

Didn't we know what would happen next?

Our first experiment with Star Drive starts an interstellar space war!

Cromwell's recall and court-martial, the frantic USSF apologies sent without benefit of reasonable translation software, and the withdrawal of all but defensive forces had no effect on the Centaurians' insane vengefulness. They fought desperate, suicidal battles to protect their residential ships. We understood those battles better once we found out that the AC's shun planets, using them exclusively for agriculture, and instead prefer to live in colonies of huge spaceships up to thirty miles long.

We were quite shocked to learn that our own solar system, only four light-years from Alpha Centauri A, is actually dwarfed by the Confederation of Centaurian Suns that surround the United System like a giant three-dimensional amoeba. Certain Centaurian leaders declared "it's high time we took Sol as well." All this led to an ever-escalating USSF presence in Alpha Centauri.

It soon became apparent that the AC's weren't in much position to make good on their threat. The superior technology of the USSF, including Stations One through Seven, gives us all the advantage, except in numbers, where the Centaurians, comprising something like forty to sixty intelligent species among their seventeen solar systems, outweigh us in soldiers and ships one hundred to one. But their Star Drive is inefficient compared to ours and better suited for leisurely transportation of supplies between solar systems than for mounting a surprise attack on Sol.

Despite the fact that they control seventeen suns, the AC's can't really threaten the United System unless we fail to keep up pressure on them, not only militarily but also with that absurd attempt to have human settlers hold captured planets for the USSF. If we withdrew entirely, in six months AC ships would no doubt start appearing outside Sol's asteroid belt. But the drain on our resources to keep up this pressure is tremendous.

I'm beginning to suspect that all Jack's ever really wanted is to blow up the main AC agricultural worlds. Our sixty-eight Xon bombs might take out twenty to thirty planets, maybe 80% of AC agricultural capacity. Famine for the AC empire, countless trillions starving to death. And maybe Jack's resented my presence all along because he knows I'd never support that. Even though maybe there's no rational alternative.

Enough. It's late and I've been babbling about the political situation to delude myself there's something I can do about it. But there's not. We've failed. And there's the matter of the shattergun on the shelf. It's all over with. I knew when Jack locked Phil up that our last chance was gone. Phil was my friend. A very level-headed guy. He kept me together the last couple weeks. Where Jack raged and snarled, Phil would just shrug and get the job done. I suppose I thought that Phil was somehow immune from conversion, that even if Jack and I went, Phil would find a way to get the *Typhoon* to Station One, outfit a new crew, and take final steps to end the war in Alpha Centauri.

I feel like I'm writing Phil's obituary. More so than my own, or Jack's. I expected Phil to triumph. I don't know why. He was more than a friend to me, he was an example of kindness, calm competence, and courage. No, there wasn't anything sexual between us, though it was painfully obvious he wanted that. But he respected my relationship to Jack and never tried to press me. I'll admit I thought of him a few times, especially these last few weeks when Jack's refusal to talk to me had worn me down to nothing, but I knew it would be folly and would destroy the beautiful friendship we had. Phil was a good man and I can only hope that despite his conversion, a tiny corner of his goodness lives on deep within him.

And here I am crying. I haven't cried when writing about Jack, and the end of a dream of romance, but here I am crying about Phil. The loss of Phil's mind. The loss of his soul. I can't believe he's gone. If I see Jack converted, will I feel the same? Or do I assume that because Jack's already so messed up, conversion will be less a tragedy?

And what the hell, Jack. Do your worst. I've decided to send this through to you anyway. Here it comes.

CHAPTER TEN
Phil's Diary
Friday, March 16, 2035, 2200 hours

Hey man, I finally got some brains back together a few minutes ago after a big dose of the Head! And now I remember I promised you another diary entry. Assuming you haven't shut down the link between the Pod and the ship. If you have, I can just print out a hard copy and have Bobby take it over to you later.

You know, Jack, when you first shoved me in here yesterday I was feeling pretty upset about the whole thing. I mean, I wasn't sure if I really was Converting when I was writing last night's entry, but you said I was and you know best after all. But what I wanted to tell you was this: I got my final dose of Conversion just this evening! I mean, I've been talking to Rogers and Pollard and the rest all day now, but not till tonight did I *feel* what they were saying. Jack, you ought to come to the Pod yourself now and just chat a bit. Not only would you see Conversion's really no big deal--it's just sort of an initiation rite into the higher mysteries of Being--but you'd also calm down some of these hotheads over here who want you to turn the ship around for Sol immediately.

See, I don't agree with them in that respect. I think we should continue to cruise the galaxy, running into supply ships every so often and taking on just enough to keep us going. We just meditate on the Head. Maybe we Convert some planets we find. The view of the stars from the Pod windows is so lovely, Jack. Why didn't we spend more time down here before? We're coming up to the Kingdoms of the Head now, the vast AC Empire. Their stars are particularly beautiful tonight.

I know my last entry didn't convince you of anything, mainly because your reaction was to pull your gun and lock me in the Pod. I can understand that, I guess. Except that consider this, Jack: *now I love the Pod*. I've changed! You could change too! You could finally relax, man. Isn't that what life is for anyway? The Emperor thinks so.

90

I know I hated the idea of the Head before. I remember calling it "the anthill, the beehive," and other stupid slander. It's none of those things. It's simply the feeling of connection to the universe. I'm not supposed to tell you some of this stuff until you're Converted yourself--it's part of the initiation thing, I guess--but I'm suspecting you're a bit Converted yourself and wouldn't mind hearing this. Am I right?

Okay, then, the big secret is that when you're Converted, you're in full contact with the Emperor himself. It's instantaneous, and has nothing to do with speed-of-light messages or anything like superspace radio. It's just the Head. You know the connection is there. And the Emperor is fantastic! You really just can't talk about him. It's just too holy. What a great guy, though.

How laughable all my pre-Conversion research into the Head seems now! All that time spent with the ship's library, trying to figure out what was going on, when the answers were just waiting for me down here in the Pod. Well, maybe it's not all wasted. Maybe we of the Head can put this knowledge to good use in future Conversion work.

There weren't too many articles available as I recall, and almost all of those were based on research done in the early stages of the war, before this whole sector got too damn dangerous for the ethnologists. I remember finding an article about the "connection" all AC citizens have. Now I realize that the connection is to the Emperor himself. It's not that the Emperor has to personally respond to trillions of messages each second. As near as I can place it, the Emperor deposits a vast dose of Loving Head into a special Reservoir upon which all citizens may draw, in fact, must draw, to sustain life.

Of course, in special circumstances a citizen may speak directly with the Emperor. The only drawback is that doing so mandates the death penalty. I haven't figured that one out yet. Maybe it's to preserve the Emperor's mental powers. Another possibility is that this is how any AC citizen finally dies. It's a matter of choice. You just decide it's time to "call the Emperor."

I recall another USSF journal article discussing the near

impossibility of AC's directly Converting humans. AC's can only Convert each other. Or *Include* is a better word, a word only we Initiates use. But the article mentioned the anomaly of Sam Hergs' spy who was sent to contact the Centaurians about an alliance between the Martians and Alpha Centaurians. The guy, infiltrated into the USSF as a radar operator, was apparently happily Converted to the Head, but upon return to Sol he seemed insane to the Martians and one of Hergs' lieutenants had him destroyed.

But apparently he was also intended to function as the AC concept of the Seed. That is, when the Centaurians set out to conquer and Include another race, they can't just land and start Converting. They need to find certain members of that race who might be predisposed to the Head in the first place. And once that alien becomes part of the Head, he or she can directly Convert other members of his species.

Apparently Seed-humans disposed to the Head are extremely rare, but it happened with Rogers. Rogers was the Seed and now we have a total of sixteen ready to Convert both humans and Martians to the Head. Rogers and the rest of the refugees still want to head directly for Mars and start Converting in earnest, but I say: we'll get to it eventually. I think we need to consolidate our own Conversions and cruise the galaxy for a while. Say about fifty or sixty years, really get to know each other well, really understand the concept of what it means to be a human or Martian dedicated to the Centaurian Empire. *Then* we take Mars and the United System.

Because you have to understand, Jack, that the basis of all this Conversion stuff is really Love. Our human culture is essentially male, that is, we probe outward, we don't bother to know ourselves. Whereas the AC's are female in orientation. They didn't conquer seventeen star systems, they grew organically until they *Included* seventeen star systems. Those systems *wished* to be absorbed. And now it's the turn of the United System to wish to be absorbed into the Centaurian Empire. She's chosen us, Jack! Don't you understand how incredibly erotic that is? To be *chosen* by the woman?

It was the realization of this overflowing Love that solidified my Conversion. As I told you in my entry last night, the Conversion was actually started by the same thing, that is, Love. It finally got into my head that the Centaurians loved us, that they wanted *us* in exactly the same way I want Amav!

I know it upset you last night, Jack, but I hope you've had time to think it through. After all, you've thrown her over, you certainly don't love her yourself. And even if you did, so what? Because the realization that I love Amav, that I've loved her ever since I first saw her, has compelled me to act decisively for once in my life. I must have her! That's all there is to it. And I know she wants me the same way. Last night it finally hit me that the only way Amav and I can be together is through Conversion. That's why I decided to Convert. That's right, Jack. At some point, after all the lovely tempting of the woman who desires you, after all the lovely tempting of the entire Alpha Centaurian Empire, you *decide* to Convert. Ultimately it's free will that gets you to paradise.

Yes, I decided to Convert because I couldn't stand the pain of not having Amav for another second. I was talking with her while I was working on the reactor. I kept meeting her brown eyes and thinking: does she feel the same? She can! She must! Her voice, her way of standing there, her face, her skin, her taut breasts, her intoxicating thighs, all tormented me. I couldn't stand it anymore. But I couldn't say anything. Suddenly I just knew: I only had to Convert to escape the pain. Not only would Conversion be a balm in itself, as the Martians have been beaming to us all these last few weeks, but the delicious truth was that ultimately Amav would also Convert, and we'd be together in the Pod! Jack, I can't begin to tell you how thrilled I am! The second she gets in here we'll move to a stateroom and lock it. And she'll be in my arms, and then in my bed! Jack, it'll be so wonderful!

And so what if you're already in the Pod, Converted yourself? If so, you'll understand, and let us alone. Because there's no possessiveness in the Pod. Everyone loves everyone else, physically as well as emotionally. I haven't yet had relations with the women here--Sheila, Anna, or Catherine--although they all stand close to me and contrive to touch me. Of course they want me, but (and I suppose I'm still not as fully Converted as I could be) I tell them I'm waiting for Amav, the love of my life. They don't understand, poor things. I suppose I'll have to satisfy them soon as best I can, if only to keep up morale here. But I know in my heart that once Amav comes, she and I will have a special love that will transcend mere Pod-love. We'll have an exclusive relationship that no one else may share. Not even you, Jack.

Tonight was my first really big dose of the Head. You see, there's a special ceremony that AC subjects do on important occasions, or, really, any time they feel like it. It's called Concentrating the Head. A group of three or more gradually focuses their individual connections with the Head to the point where they start a sort of mental feedback with the Head and with each other.

Now AC subjects can't actually read other AC minds as the Martians had hoped. Rather, since all enjoy a common link with the Head, we start moving toward each other, closer and closer, until we attain a sort of pseudo-mind reading. The empathic connection between AC subjects at this time is indescribable.

I'd been asleep for a couple hours after a satisfying meal of lobster, prime rib, and a couple bottles of excellent 1970s vintage Italian wine. When I woke I saw Rogers, Pollard, Emory Bell, Arnold Protor, and Will Connors relaxing in the huge leather armchairs around the coffee table. Sheila and Ben McCasland, Lee Borman, and Patrick James were off in various staterooms, as were the Martians. Joe, Anna, and Catherine talked quietly at another table on the other side of the spiral staircase leading back to the *Typhoon*.

"What's going on over there?" I asked Anna when I'd noticed a peculiar energy emanating from the five men around the coffee table.

"They're concentrating Head," she replied.

"Really?" Pollard had hinted earlier about the wonders of Concentrated Head.

"You'd be welcome to join them," Catherine said. "Or you could join me in Stateroom Eight."

I smiled at her. "No thanks. I told you I'm waiting for Amav. No hard feelings."

"No hard feelings. But why don't you join the group? Anna and Joe and I would, except that we did some Concentrated with Sheila this afternoon and are still a bit dinged by it." She patted my thigh. "Go on over."

"Well, I guess I will." I have to admit I was apprehensive. I was a neophyte to all this. I wandered over to the men around the coffee table.

"Hello, Phil," Pollard said warmly. "We were just discussing what a jerk Jack Commer really is."

His statement might have been true, but what was important was the way he said it. It was a Statement of Head, concentrated to thousands of times its normal potency. Instantly my brain was spread into a vast field of wildflowers. I smiled easily at these five men who were now all my deep and intimate friends, and I settled into another armchair. Connors poured me a coffee mug full of whiskey and I realized they'd been drinking it straight out of the bottle. But even as I sipped, I realized that the liquor wasn't one hundredth as powerful as the Head filling the space around the coffee table. How wonderful to be able to ignore the alcoholic effects of the blazing liquor and swill it like a soft drink. Bell refilled my coffee mug.

"Phil, I'm glad you're here," said Rogers. "Hopefully that means the other three will be Converting before long, and we'll finally be able to get this pile of junk aimed at the United System."

"But we're also glad that you're here, because we like you so much," Arbold Protor put in. "I really thought Jack was going to shoot you last night when he pushed you in here."

"He wouldn't shoot a fellow USSF'er," Connors said. "Right, Phil?"

"Yeah. Will, I wish you'd convinced me to come over here earlier."

"We were all so uptight. I can't understand why Jack is

holding out."

"Because he's a malevolent jerk," Rogers said.

"But once he's Converted, he'll be your best friend," Connors said. "I guarantee it."

"Aaah," said Rogers. "I hate the mother."

"He's really not so bad."

"The dude's obsessed. He wants to shoot all of us. I mean, if he'd just allow us to talk to him, talk some sense into him, but no way. He's gotta keep us locked up in the Pod here."

"Hey, you don't realize what a great thing you've got here in the Pod," I said.

"If he'd only realize about the Head," Connors said.

"You guys are just trying to rationalize," Rogers came back. "You're still loyal to him, even though he's the enemy. I'm especially surprised at you, Connors. You've been over here quite a while now."

"Hey, man, I'm in touch with the Head," Connors said. "All I'm saying is that no human can be our enemy now. They're just yet to be Converted, that's all."

"But Bobby's the enemy," Protor put in. He set his drink down on the table and leaned back. "Bobby won't Convert. I don't know why. He can't be Included."

"Maybe Commer's the same way," Rogers said. "Maybe they'll have to be *taken care of* somehow."

There was silence. Pollard looked up at me. "How about this Amav woman? Will she Convert?"

"Oh, yes, yes of course," I gulped, realizing that Rogers and Pollard had just threatened three people's lives. If it were true that some people couldn't be Converted, I now understood in horror, they'd have to be killed. Or else they'd find a way to kill us. "Of course Amav will join us. Soon. I can feel it. Jack too. He'll come over. Probably Bobby after that."

"He doesn't know what he's talking about," Rogers said.

"But remember we originally thought Phil was Unconvertible as well," Connors said. "Maybe some people are just harder than others."

"But that makes them dangerous. Damn dangerous." Rogers

paused for a gulp of whiskey. "Maybe even more dangerous than we've wanted to believe." His eyes settled on me again. "So what's to stop Jack Commer from jettisoning this Pod any time he feels like it?"

"Well, it could be done. But he wouldn't."

"Besides, we'd just drift to Alpha Centauri right alongside the *Typhoon,*" Connors said. "We have our own air and supplies, and backup generators."

"Then what's to stop Commer from vaporizing us with one of the PlanetBlasters?"

Everyone looked puzzled. Finally Connors said: "Hell, maybe he would do it. I don't know. Why hasn't he before?"

"His old crewmembers. His brother," Protor said.

"Maybe," Rogers said. "But how long is that gonna hold him? The dude's obsessed, man. Sooner or later he'll decide to off us. And he has all the weapons now."

We all pondered this statement. I was getting a bit edgy despite the Head everywhere, and I was glad when Bell said: "Hey, we're losing the high, man, talkin' about all this gloomy stuff. Let's Concentrate a little more, okay?"

"Yeah, fine," said Pollard. "Now we've got Phil to work with. Just relax and follow our lead. Mix in your energy when you feel ready."

I took a deep breath and became more aware of my surroundings. Overhead two bright red reflector lamps bathed us in grainy surreal crimson. The lights reflected off the black table as two red-yellow orbs. The room around us was quiet except for the sounds of Joe, Anna, and Catherine giggling on the other side of the room, entwined on a huge couch with their clothes off, pawing each other like kittens. Patrick James wandered with his hands in his pockets, staring at the ceiling. Sheila was in one of the big conference rooms, looking out a window at the stars.

I sighed. I'd escaped to a better world. Those of us in the Pod were soldiers with a special camaraderie, fighting to establish the primacy of the Head throughout the galaxy. I gasped, because this was indeed the goal. Galaxy-wide domination! I met Connors' eyes and felt a surge of powerful

Head. I was directly participating in the Head Field! All you had to do was look into another's eyes and feel the resonance. I turned to Bell, to Rogers, to Pollard and Protor, each time getting higher and higher on the Head. These men knew their soldierly tools well. Our world floated in delicious red fantasy.

"We've got to establish a plan," Rogers said. "We've been muddling around for a while, gaining Converts, but we haven't had a plan. Exactly what are we going to do to make sure Commer Converts? Or supposing he doesn't Convert and has to be dealt with another way?"

"Who knows?" Protor said. "We'll let the Head decide."

"I say we've got to know how we'll act when the time comes. That way we'll be prepared when the Head finally tells us to proceed. I think we've been damn ignorant of what's going on in the *Typhoon,* if you ask me." Rogers turned to me. "Okay, Phil, you were the last person in the ship. What's Commer's state of mind? Is he gonna Convert? Or are we gonna have to waste him?"

I sat back, numb. I saw his point clearly. Either Jack Commer was going to Convert, or Jack Commer would have to be eliminated. The threat of an Unconverted aboard the ship couldn't be tolerated. Nevertheless I couldn't imagine really doing it. "Well, I'm sure hoping he'll Convert. He isn't stable right now. The last time I talked to him he was almost out of his mind with paranoia. He thinks *Amav's* out to get him, that she's the greater danger to him than *we* are. Can you believe that?" I chuckled nervously. Strange you can get so blissfully blasted on the Head and still be nervous.

"So you think because he's unstable, he'll Convert soon? I think the opposite. That he's getting unstable enough to jettison the Pod and let loose with a PlanetBlaster."

"Wow!" Emory Bell laughed. "Can you imagine what it'd be *like?* We feel ourselves jettisoned! Our gravity cuts off because we aren't running off the main drive anymore! We're floating around, and then we feel the laser blow open the side of the ship! In a microsecond we're all blown out into space! God!" And he went on to more hysterical laughing.

Rogers waved at Bell in disgust. "I tell you, we've got to act *now*."

"Act now?" I said. "And do what?"

Rogers shrugged. "Off him before he offs us."

I looked away. Protor said: "Now look, Carl, maybe there's another way. Now I was just sitting here having this tremendous insight."

"Yeah?"

"And I was thinking--I was realizing--that this ship we're on, both the Pod and the *Typhoon,* is sacred. Our mission is *sacred.* The Head's not going to allow it to fail. It's not going to allow Jack Commer to get out of control."

"Forget it. Commer's not under control of the Head. He's still a random factor."

"All I'm saying is that the Head may be maneuvering in ways we don't understand. Maybe Commer's mental disorder is the beginning of part of the Head's plan. I mean, this ship is a magnet of Head Energy. Surely the Head knows everything that's going on here now."

"I'll vouch for that," Bell put in.

"Me, too," Connors said. "The Emperor knows we're here!"

I began forming images of vectors of mental power extending through space, surrounding our ship, emanating from the Emperor himself. It was true. We'd be protected. Jack Commer would be no threat to us. I sighed with relief.

"God, I thought we were all gonna hafta die," I said.

"No," Protor said. "The Head knows we're here. The Head will make peace between Sol and Alpha Centauri. In the same way that, even though we're totally different from the Centaurians, we've become friends with them, so all beings will become friends with the Centaurians and with each other. The Head will see to that. Just think, Phil, Earthmen and Centaurians will see they have no real differences after all, that after the initial pain of coming into contact with alien cultures, we'll all dwell as one in the Head. And you and I, and the rest of us, will play a significant role in this new understanding."

"Wow," I muttered. The idea of us playing a crucial role in

ending this exhausting war with the Centaurians, the idea of a battle of alien cultures culminating in an erotic burst of understanding and love, was overwhelming. Graceful lines of psychic power traced themselves in the thin red fantasy fog above our group of soldiers. A heating vent on the ceiling came to life. I hadn't realized I'd been shivering all this time, but now I was bathed in hot nourishing air.

No enemies, just misunderstandings to clear up! I knew that you, Jack, would discover this at the proper time. Amav would, and Bobby would. Amav would be mine! All beings would live in peace, and whatever they desired would be theirs! This war had been so foolish, the history of our race had been so foolish, so full of *wanting* but not *getting,* all because we didn't have the Head. We didn't know *how* to get what we wanted.

"Yeah …" Bell murmured. "I always knew there was no problem."

"Damn right," Pollard said. "That's the way it's always been, you know. People get uptight, they make up all sorts of problems. But really, there's no problem. You just have to get to the point where you see that."

"Yeah …" I sighed gratefully. "How many years has it taken me to *see* that?"

"Yeah, but look at Commer," Rogers said. "That guy's a textbook example of someone with all sorts of problems. He might just screw the whole deal up for all of us."

"But not for the Head as a whole, even if he did screw us up," Protor said. "Remember that it's a historical necessity for the Head to conquer the galaxy."

"Sure, but where does that get us? We get killed and never get to have Head parties like this ever again. Besides, even if the Head will ultimately triumph, Commer could hold it up for years maybe. Hundreds of years maybe, by wiping out our cell. A cell of human and Martian Converteds isn't easy to come by, you know. Think of how many billions of beings will suffer for those hundreds of years because we weren't around to do our part for the Head."

We all sat digesting this.

"Yeah, so he's in the way of the Head," Connors said. "He's gotta Convert any day now."

"I'm saying events have overtaken us," Rogers replied. "We can't wait even a few hours, really. He could wipe us out at any time. We needed Phil in here to work on the engine when it comes time for us to fly to Earth. We had to wait that long, I guess, for Phil to Convert. But the point is that we don't need Jack Commer in here. I think we're just going to have to kill him before he kills us."

"Wow …" Connors said.

"I know you're with the Head in this matter, Will," Rogers said. "Don't pretend doubt out of loyalty to your former master."

Connors shook his head. "N-no, I can see your point."

I stared at Rogers. I've fought in Alpha Centauri, I've used blasters that wiped out star cruisers, but I've never sat in on a session where someone has just quietly plotted another person's murder.

"It'll be Pollard and me," Rogers said "Later tonight."

"You don't have weapons," I pointed out hopefully. Surely they'd have to call this thing off, necessary as it was.

"With the Head, I can do anything. Pollard and I'll take some of the kitchen knives. We'll carve the dude *up*."

"I'm sure he changed the access codes since I Converted. And if you try to disable the system, he's got the ship's entrance wired so you'll get fried."

Rogers probed into my eyes until my Head level escalated giddily to thousands of times its former height. But I descended rapidly. Evidently a human being can only stand that sort of Head for seconds at a time. I came out of it woozily.

"You," Rogers said evenly, "will disable the hatch blasters for us."

"Me?"

"Yes, you. Just hack into the codes and disable them."

"We know you can do it," Pollard said. "You know you *have* to do it."

"You'll disable them at the last minute, so Commer won't get wise," Rogers said. "Then we'll rush up to the Control Room and slice the mother to pieces. We'll do it at three in the morning. You'll disable the hatch security at 2:30."

"Well, okay …" I whispered. "That'll be … okay."

"All right, then. I'm gonna catch a little rest before then. It's 9:15 now. Nate, I'll see you and Phil at the staircase at 2:30."

"Yeah, right," Pollard said. "See you then."

"See you," I mumbled.

Rogers disappeared into one of the staterooms. "My God!" Emory Bell said. "Nate, are you and Carl really going to kill the guy?"

"I think we have to, Emory," Pollard said. "I think Carl's right. Commer's too much a risk right now."

"But that's not the way of the Head!"

"Yeah, but sometimes," Protor put in, "even the Head has to be a little cruel. I'm afraid Nate and Carl are right, Emory. We can't let Commer cause hundreds of years of suffering to billions of innocent beings."

Pollard stood up. "I'm gonna rest a while, too. Need my energy later on. See you guys."

The others stood and took their leave. The Concentrated Head was diminishing, though my own mind still surged. But I was depressingly aware that no new Head would be added from the outside.

Connors came over as I sat dumbfounded in my armchair. "Kinda weird, isn't it, Phil?"

"Yeah, I guess so."

"I guess it's not so bad, really. I mean, everyone has to die sometime, right? So it's no big loss, I guess."

"No, I can see the necessity for it, I suppose."

"All the same, maybe we'd better not tell Joe. Or even Borman or Pat."

"Yeah, that's a good idea."

"See you, man." Connors went to the windows and put his arms around Sheila. She turned enthusiastically for a kiss. I looked away. The way the two had melted into each other reminded me painfully of Amav. God, I hoped she wouldn't take the death of her husband too seriously. Surely, once she

Converted, she'd see the necessity. God, I wanted her. I was high on Concentrated Head and I had to share it with Amav.

But I shivered with anxiety. What if she didn't want me? What if she wanted Connors or even Rogers? And I was aching so badly for her! But at that exact moment of Concentrated Head despair I caught sight of a magazine on the shelf under the coffee table. I'd been subliminally aware of it all along, and now, in my moment of deepest unease, I returned to it.

It was the January issue of *Spacegirls*. How had this come to my consciousness at this second? It had to be a gift from the Head. The Head had to be saying to me: *Phil, don't worry, calm down, everything's all right!* I knew the magazine was morphine for my wounds, that it was artificial, that it wasn't the answer, and yet, it *was* the answer. *Spacegirls* was a manifestation of the Head, even as part of me knew it was just Borman's subscription we all used to laugh about.

Women. How could such creatures possibly exist? How could they be so beautiful and exciting? This question had tormented me all my life. What kind of a God would create women? Their eyes, their smiles, their hair, their breasts and asses and thighs? Was it an infinitely wise God, or a cruel God? It had to be a wise God! For women were the soul of this universe. And Amav was the premier example of what a woman should be. A God who could create Amav, or any woman, had to be in love with his own universe. And as I looked over a ten-page spread about Carolyn, a secretary on New Luna, I understood why. Carolyn was astonishing, slender, with perfect firm tits, long dark hair and an amusing, intelligent, oval face. Brown eyes that looked right through me. And then there was that black, tight-fitting Eros 12 spacesuit she paraded in peek-a-boo poses, stripping it off inch by inch.

And why was Carolyn so apocalyptically beautiful? Because she was Amav's twin sister! Her face was similar, her eyes close, her hair exactly the same, her stance the same. My heart leapt to understand that Carolyn's breasts had to be exactly the same as Amav's! It didn't matter that the editors of *Spacegirls* were using me, jerking me through their masturbatory little story page by page as Carolyn got progressively nuder, then widened her legs and finally jammed her lovely butt right into the camera lens, her fingers exploring everywhere. No, the editors had read my soul perfectly. In fact, they had to be agents of the Head. They'd united me with Carolyn, united me with Amav. They'd foretold the union of Alpha Centauri and Sol. After all these months of my tormented need for Amav, I found that the editors had known all along to bring her to me. They'd done an outstanding job. I stood. The Pod pulsated with the desire for union.

"Hey, Phil," came a soft voice. I turned to a naked woman.

"Carolyn!" I gasped.

She blinked. "Catherine," she said, drawing back.

"I've got to have you, Carolyn! Come here!"

"No, come over with Anna and Joe and me, darling."

"No, gotta have you *now!* Carolyn! Oh, Carolyn!"

"Phil, my name is *Catherine!*"

"Amav!"

"No, I'm not Amav either!" But then she laughed. "What the hell, if you want me to be Amav, I'll be Amav! Okay?"

"Be Carolyn too!" And I took her into my arms.

And a long time afterwards, as I lay alone in my stateroom spiraling out of Concentrated Head, knowing that all my desires would be taken care of throughout eternity, I began to start thinking about you again, Jack. My old pal Jack. That maybe I should tell you the whole story of this evening. Have you been listening? You know, I can't believe that Rogers and Pollard mean to go through with their ridiculous plan. Ultimately the Head will stop them. Because the Head wants you on our side. Consider it, Jack. Come to the Head. Be Included with us. You'll get what you want throughout eternity. You'll unite with your own personal Carolyn, or Catherine, as the case may be.

But I have to go now. Rogers is pounding on my door. It's 0230 hours, for God's sake. Says he has to talk to me. Bye for now. Sending this entry through. Yes, I have enough backdoor codes to get into your email system, and any other systems I want to.

CHAPTER ELEVEN
Bobby's Diary
Friday, March 16, 2035, 2200 hours

The nine-hundred-foot-long colonizing ship *Pegasus* orbited dead planet Argus IV in the year 2466. Billy Johnson, Ship's Historian, checked data coming from the planet's surface. "Hmm," he said. "Looks like Argus IV once harbored a race of beings far more advanced than humans. Evidently they killed themselves in a gigantic bacteriological war. I'd better report to the Captain."

Billy entered the Control Room in the nose of the *Pegasus*. Captain Jack Cramer swiveled around in his chair. Beyond the cockpit window lay the curved blue horizon of Argus IV from one hundred miles up. "What is it, Johnson?" Cramer snapped irritably. "Can't you see I'm busy?"

"I'm sorry to disturb you, sir, but I've just discovered that Argus IV was once populated by beings who are now extinct. There are traces of ancient cities and highways. It looks as if they killed themselves with bacteriological weapons. The whole surface is contaminated with deadly bacteria."

"Hmm. How do you know it's deadly?"

"Well, according to the computer analysis--"

"The computer can be wrong," Cramer cut in. "I say we're going to land on Argus IV anyway. We've been in space for months now and need to land. We have three hundred colonists who can easily clean up any bacteria they might find. That is all. Dismissed."

"Sir, if I might point out, we will all die if we land on Argus IV. It cannot be colonized by humans."

"Johnson, you are out of line. And anyway, how come you, the historian, are reporting this to me? Why not the science department?"

"They haven't known where to look for the ruins. And they didn't want to worry you about the bacteria anyway."

"I'm sure they know what's best. You had best keep to your own specialty, Johnson."

"Uh, yes, sir."

"Johnson, you're only twelve years old, is that right?"

"Yes, sir. But I did score 98 on my Space Force Entrance Exam."

"I know, I know. It's just that I don't favor letting twelve-year-olds into the service."

"Well, they made an exception because of my background, sir, I guess."

"I know, I know." Cramer picked a comm off his desk and paged through it. "You were transported through time from the era of the American Civil War to the year 2464. For the last two years you've been in the Space Academy and just graduated before this mission started three months ago."

"Evidently they thought my knowledge of the past would be useful here."

"I disagree. I don't care what era you're from. All I know is that you spend all your time writing stories about the Civil War! I for one am sick of it! When you do take a break from that, you're prophesying disaster on Argus IV! Well, I'm telling you, no more Civil War stories, no more bacteria scares, no more nothing! Stick to your own work, which is documenting the history of this mission!"

Billy took a deep breath. "Sir, I feel I must tell you that I've decided that the time has come to report everything to you as honestly as I can. My previous reports have been trying to cover up the situation, but I now must tell you that we are doomed if we land on Argus IV."

"So noted," Cramer yawned. "You know, Johnson, you're as bad as that other twelve-year-old I got stuck with--what's her name, Angela Emerson. She was openly telling everyone our mission would fail! So I confined her to her quarters. Not that we'd miss a Ship's Artist anyway." He paged through his comm, then flung it on the console. "And *she's* from England in the 1820s! Why can't people just stay in their own era? We can't afford to constantly be taking new people into the twenty-fifth century!"

"Sir, may I point out that the Federation's Colonization

Policy explicitly recommends--"

"No, you may not point that out! And furthermore--"

Just then a buzzer sounded and a red light flashed. Cramer reached behind him and snapped the buzzer switch off, shouting: "And furthermore, I won't have traitors on my ship! When we unload the colonists on Argus IV, you and Angela will stay with them! I don't need your constant--"

"Sir, may I point out--"

"No, you may not point out!"

"Sir, the warning buzzer you just turned off is the Meteor Shower Alert System."

"Wha--?" Cramer turned back to the console and looked at his main scanner. But by now he no longer needed to consult it.

Hundreds of glowing red meteors were heading directly for the ship.

Jack Cramer never knew what hit him.

A meteor the size of an American Civil War cannon ball tore through the huge window in a dazzling explosion and instantly blasted Cramer into a thousand pieces of bloody guts.

As other meteors streaked through the Control Room, twisting it to unrecognizable scrap metal in milliseconds, Billy was flung backwards and down a flight of stairs. Meteors screamed through the ship four feet above his head, churning down the length of the ship, blowing the ship's air into space.

In fact, wind was being sucked around him at hundreds of miles per hour. Gasping, Billy groped for a storage locker next to him and pulled out a spacesuit.

It wasn't one of the regular bulky spacesuits that could keep you alive for weeks in deep space, but one of the new tight-fitting models Billy had never worn before. He quickly got into the black suit and zipped it up, trying not to think of the older boys who'd been passing around an issue of *Spacegirls* where one of the women was taking off just this kind of spacesuit. Her name was Carolyn and she was from New Luna. The boys had made cracks about "bulging crotches," and when he sneaked a look at that *Spacegirls,* Billy knew what they were talking about. Billy had once seen a man and a woman go off for a spacewalk in these tight black suits. The woman's suit was so form-fitting that Billy had been shocked. The man and woman had come back in a few minutes gasping about the view of the stars and the joy of being weightless. There'd been something suspicious about them Billy couldn't figure out.

Now Billy turned on his suit's energy resonator, which created a force field around his head. Normally this suit was intended for use on planetary surfaces where the suit would process the outer atmosphere and convert it to breathable air, but the suit held enough air for a half-hour spacewalk and kept you pressurized even without a helmet. Of course, there was no joy in being weightless now. The artificial gravity controls had been destroyed and now even the last lights went out. Billy felt the ship lurching as ever more meteors smashed into it. If people were screaming, if they were crying for help, no one could hear, because the atmosphere was all gone. All Billy could hear was the whir of tiny blowers bringing fresh air into the force field around his head.

So the suit worked. Billy was glad to be alive. He was puzzled this suit fit so well. It was comfortably snug but gave complete freedom of movement.

There was only one possibility open to him, the small hangar of exploration craft below. There was a larger berth of lifeboat craft at the far end of the *Pegasus,* but he knew he'd never make the journey down the crumpled length of the ship.

He swung down a stairwell. His suit flashlight revealed only small holes here. Maybe the main mass of meteors had plunged through the upper levels of the ship, while smaller stragglers had pierced the lower sections, doing less damage. Whenever he touched the walls or the railing Billy could feel the vibrations of the ship tearing itself apart. He could also feel the fresh pings of new meteors striking home.

He made it to the small hangar open to the cloud surface a hundred miles below, rotating crazily due to the ship's gyrations. Six one-man exploration ships were clamped to steel supports in three columns of two ships each. But the middle and right columns of ships had been blasted by meteors. Billy could see a small figure working on the canopy of one of the ships in the left column. He shined his flashlight down.

The figure turned. It was Angela. A return splash of light came from her flashlight. He pulled himself down reverberating girders and spoke through his suit microphone: "Angela! I thought you were confined to quarters on E deck!"

"Billy, you're safe! Well, I *was* confined to quarters," Angela said, opening the canopy of the exploration craft as Billy moved to the one behind it, "but when I heard those meteors coming through the ship I headed for the lifeboats. But Billy, I never made it there. I think the whole rear of the ship broke off. I saw something huge drifting back there when I was putting on this suit."

"The colonists' living quarters--the lifeboats--all gone," Billy muttered. "So these are the last two escape craft left." But he found himself staring at Angela's black suit. It was as tight on her as that woman's had been.

"We may be the last people left," Angela said, looking away from Billy's staring. She settled into her ship and tested the controls.

Billy also looked away. "I know. I saw Cramer die. And the biggest meteors probably went right through the officer's quarters." He got into his own ship.

"Where are we going? The planet?"

"You know we have to. These ships could never make it to even another planet, let alone another solar system. But listen, I discovered all sorts of bacteria down there. We'll have to keep these suits on. I don't know how much good they'll do, though."

Angela nodded. "We'll both just have to take our chances." She secured her canopy and made her final countdown. "Five--four--three--two--one--drop!" she called, and Billy watched her jettison perfectly. She fired her retro rockets to cut her speed and begin the spiral down to the planet's surface. She was an excellent pilot. After all, she and Billy had been tied for first place in piloting and navigation at the Space Academy. He watched Angela fading from sight and completed his own checks.

The dying *Pegasus* swung violently. Billy looked out the open hanger doors to see that the ship had indeed broken in two. The ruined rear floated a mile behind. Debris drifted everywhere. It was a regular junkyard up here.

Billy closed his canopy, pressurized the cockpit, warmed up the engine, and quickly made his countdown. He hit the DROP button. Nothing happened. He hit the button again and again. And when he looked around, he got the shock of his life. The planet below was gone. There was nothing but blackness. It took him a few panicky moments to realize that *Pegasus* was twisting on all three axes now. He felt a long, terrifying vibration and realized that the rest of the ship was breaking up.

The planet came into view again, impossibly blinding. He shielded his eyes and tried to make sense of what was going on. He ran through his checks. The engine was operating perfectly. The air was holding. All thrusters were operational. But the steel clamps holding the tiny ship to its berth refused to release. Finally Billy depressurized, opened the canopy, and surveyed the situation. Now he saw that the ejector mechanism was progressively buckling as more and more pressure was brought upon it by a steadily deforming girder. Several thousand tons of whirling, shredded spaceship were warping whatever structures remained.

Grimly Bill searched for the ship's emergency toolbox and set to work unbolting the ejector mechanism and the locking clamps. Long minutes later the escape ship floated free in its berth. Billy got inside, pushed off with his hands, and closed the canopy.

He spent a couple more minutes using thrusters to stabilize his ship, then fired his retro rockets and felt the reverse acceleration build up. Gravity increased to several times its normal force.

Far above him the *Pegasus* exploded.

He looked at his watch. Half an hour had passed since Angela dropped out.

Billy realized that, given *Pegasus'* hour-long orbit of the planet, she and Billy would land on opposite sides of Argus IV.

The exploration ships weren't designed to cruise through a planetary atmosphere, and the most Angela and Billy could hope for would be to follow their spiraling paths down to a safe landing.

Billy turned the ship around so its nose pointed to the ground. Soon the canopy flared red as the ship was enveloped in a miles-long trailer of friction fire. The onboard computer held the slender ship steady and calculated the correct moment for deployment of several sets of parachutes stored for just this sort of emergency landing.

The parachutes shot out, one after the other, wrenching Billy forward in his seat. Finally the ship drifted under the final three parachutes, then hit the surface of the planet at forty miles per hour and knocked Billy cold.

He woke up hours later in the twilight of the Argus IV day to notice that his ship had broken into several large pieces and that he lay on bright yellow sand.

He was stranded on an alien world. All ship's instruments were smashed. But the smooth black skin of his spacesuit was intact, and the force field still worked. The energy resonator, powered by its tiny nuclear reactor, was converting the Argus IV atmosphere into air and efficiently processing waste products. The only thing Bobby needed was food and water, and if these could be found, they could be processed through the sterilization kit from the craft and passed through the force field to his mouth.

But what had happened to Angela? Had she survived? And how was she doing on the other side of this planet? Somehow Billy knew he would find her. They each had these miracle spacesuits that could keep them alive.

The glossy black surface of Billy's suit was only a sixteenth of an inch thick and was shaped to every contour of his body. He could see the outlines of his biceps, his legs, his hips. Angela probably hadn't fully seen this suit in all the confusion in the hangar. He wondered how she would react to seeing him now.

Billy stood up. He was on an unexplored planet at twilight. On the eastern horizon--he called it east, because the sun was setting in the opposite direction--dark purple columns and arches, remnants of a dead civilization, glowed in the last rays of the sun. Billy took some supplies from his wrecked escape ship and strode across the fluorescent yellow sand. Angela was somewhere out in that night. He would explore the ruins of this world on the way and sooner or later he would find her.

*

"Well, imagine running into *you,*" came the voice over Billy's suit radio. There was Angela, in her glossy black suit, stepping over the shattered blocks of yet another alien coliseum. Her hair had grown very long.

"Angela!" Billy said. "I've been looking for you for weeks. Or is it months?"

"I've lost track myself. But I knew to walk in this direction."

"And it's good that we decided to walk *towards* each other. Otherwise we'd be walking around this world forever."

Angela stood before Billy. "Somehow I knew to walk to the west. But we both knew we'd find each other. We had to. We're the only survivors, after all. I knew you'd get out. You must've had a delay."

"Y-yes …" Billy said, again aware of just how form-fitting Angela's spacesuit was. And now that he saw her in full sunshine, he was even more shocked. The suit clearly showed everything tightly outlined in smooth black plastic. Billy had never noticed it before, but Angela was really quite well-developed. Against his will he thought about Carolyn unzipping her spacesuit down the front. "Well," he gulped, "my ship got stuck. I had to unbolt it myself. Then the *Pegasus* broke up. I had enough trouble getting out in one piece."

Angela sat down next to Billy on a broken column. "This world seems to be one big desert. Did you see any oceans?"

"No, nothing but this sand and these ruined cities. But I see you must've solved the food and water problem the same way I did."

"The animals. I called them water creatures."

"Funny, so did I." It had been a miraculous find. The flesh

of the small, easily captured water creatures had proved fully nourishing, and instead of blood, the creatures had fresh water running through their veins. How they got this water from a desert world was a mystery to Billy. But eating them gave incredible bursts of energy. Billy had often run for an entire day without tiring. "I figured that passing anything through the force field should automatically sterilize it," he went on. "So eating them was okay. I don't think we've been exposed to any of the bacteria."

"I figured that out, too."

Billy saw Angela looking down at his hard thighs outlined in the tight spacesuit. She caught his glance and turned away. Billy focused on the sand. "I found out that this entire planet is covered with deadly bacteria from a war centuries ago. I should have told you more about that before we escaped. I'm sorry."

"That's no problem." Angela looked directly into his eyes. Billy was surprised that she had brown eyes. He'd never noticed them before. Her freckled face, with brown eyes framed by that long, dark, shiny hair, was really very pretty. "We both knew we'd find each other, and that nothing bad was going to happen to either of us. Landing on opposite sides of the planet was just a big inconvenience, that's all. We're not going to let a bunch of silly bacteria stop us."

Stop us? Billy wondered. *From doing what?* "You're not upset? By all this?" Now he stole a glance at her slender glossy black legs. Then looked up to meet her eyes again. They both turned away.

"No, I'm not upset. Just the opposite." Angela smiled at the ground.

Billy was stunned. Did she like him? What would happen if he tried to kiss her? Could he do that?

But it was impossible anyway. They'd have to turn off the force fields. For a long time Billy watched his feet play with the dust. He couldn't say a word.

The silence got more and more awkward. Finally Angela said: "It sure is weird always hearing you over the radio."

Billy felt hot. There was pressure on his shoulder, then

against his force field. Angela leaned in, merging the force fields, and her pure voice came: "See? Did you know you could talk by merging fields like this?"

"I knew that, I guess …" he stammered. She smelled wonderful, her face two inches from his. She was smiling.

He shakily put his arm around her and she immediately wrapped herself around him. He kissed her on the cheek, then found her lips. He was surprised how soft they were. Billy kissed her again and again, unable to think about it ever ending. He fell backwards with Angela atop him.

Then the force fields came apart. Angela straightened up. "Are you mad at me?" he blurted.

Angela put her hand through her own force field to smooth her hair. "No, silly."

"Do … you like me?"

"Of course I like you, Billy."

"Well, I like you, but … what does that mean?"

"We can worry about all that later," Angela laughed. "Kiss me now."

The force fields merged again. Her gloved hand gripped his bicep tightly, and Billy could feel each of her fingers through his suit. He began to think about why the adults had gone outside the *Pegasus* in these suits, one man and one woman at a time.

"Billy …" Angela whispered as they broke off for air. "We walked around this world, in opposite directions, so we could be *together*."

Billy nodded. "You're right. The old race ruined it, but it's ours now."

"Our planet …" Again she looked to his thighs. "You know, I've actually taken off my suit a few times. You know, to clean up and all. Even though there's no water, you can sort of just let the wind wash all over you for an hour or so."

"Really? Really?" Billy gasped, unable to believe she'd actually said that. Not daring to picture it. The wind, flowing over Carolyn's breasts? "But what about the bacteria? I mean, I never took mine off. I just trusted the internal cleaning filters on the suit to take care of everything."

"Well, maybe the bacteria gets counteracted by the water creatures somehow. All I know is I've felt perfectly fine since I started eating them." She touched her wrist bracelet and shut down her force field. In two quick motions she yanked her gloves off.

"*No!*" Billy cried, staring at her small naked fingers.

"Well, it *is* our planet," Angela murmured. Billy felt her touch the switch at his own wrist. His energy resonator clicked off and the cool dry breeze of the planet was in his hair. Angela's lips were on his own and then she was on top of him.

"It's our planet now!" she whispered fiercely. "It *is!*"

CHAPTER TWELVE
Daily Addendum by Ship's Captain
Saturday, March 17, 2035, 0300 hours

I have read the diary entries of the *Typhoon* crew/passengers for 3/16/35. I completely discount Amav's paranoia and also Sperry's addled threats against my person. I find both these persons insane. While not yet converted, as far as I can tell, Amav can be expected to follow her lover Sperry into the pod momentarily. I find her histrionics about committing suicide before allowing her conversion to be merely a not-very-clever attempt to disguise the fact that she is already in a pre-conversion state.

As for Bobby, I have to shake my head at his sudden veer into insanity. Whether or not he converts to the Centaurians doesn't really matter at this stage, but I knew his Civil War obsession was the beginning of the end, and I tried my mightiest to get him to shake that. Instead, he chose to go insane. His rather pornographic conclusion clearly shows that he has gone over the edge.

I, Jack Commer, have gotten control over myself. My earlier diary entry for 3/16 showed some of the emotional strain I've been through recently, but I will let it stand. This addendum is to state for the record that I have overcome those emotions by a process of rational thinking. I've decided to simply barricade myself in the Control Room and never come out again. I'll let Amav and Bobby have the run of the ship, whether they're converted or not. They won't contaminate me in here. When my food supplies run out, I'll either simply starve to death, or end it all quickly with a shot from the shattergun at my belt. Or perhaps I'll simply vaporize myself with my USSF blaster. All the accounts say this is far less painful than being shattered.

I rationally understand that these are the meandering thoughts of a man who, having failed completely in his mission, goes about tidying up his business at the end, simply because he has nothing better to do.

For the good of my psyche, and to allow no more pollution

in the ship's record, I will allow no more diary entries from any crew/passengers. I am going to write this on a star map and post it on the bulletin board in the kitchenette. This will be my last excursion into the remainder of the ship. Specifically, this is designed to let Amav and Bobby know that I will accept no more of their emailed filth or any other form of communication.

I also give my solemn pledge never again to utter a word to any human being.

CHAPTER THIRTEEN
This is Strictly a Family Matter!

THERE WILL BE NO MORE DIARY ENTRIES SUBMITTED IN ANY MANNER WHATSOEVER TO THE CONTROL ROOM. JACK COMMER, SUPREME COMMANDER, USSF. 3/17/35, 0310 HOURS.

Jack had always known these three-foot-wide paper star maps would come in handy someday. Joe was always after him to trash them, but hell, you could write letters four inches high on the back. Yeah, this looked good. This got the damn message across.

Jack opened the Control Room hatch to the harsh white of the fuselage. He needed just a second to step down the catwalk to the kitchenette, staple the notice to the ship's bulletin board, and maybe head down the ladder for a quick stop at the lavatory.

Well, he hadn't considered *that* angle. Once he locked himself in the Control Room, he'd have to use the emergency port-a-toilet and keep throwing disintegration cubes into the pot. Probably a few sanitizer cubes wouldn't hurt, either. He could stock up on these in the kitchenette. And then one last trip to a normal bathroom, the last in his life.

Briefly Jack toyed with the idea of blasting his head off so as to avoid ever having to use the port-a-toilet. He shook his head feverishly. This whole mission was so confusing, so complicated and foul.

Just as he was stepping out onto the catwalk, he heard the buzz of the intercom.

"*Forget it,*" he hissed. "I talk to no one! Ever again!"

"Jack," came Amav's voice. "Jack, I know you don't want to talk, but--"

"*No one,*" he muttered. "Not you, not anyone. *Ever.*"

"Jack, can you hear me? This is serious. I'm in the Sensor Room."

Jack froze. The Sensor Room was just a few steps ahead. The door was open.

"Jack, I saw something strange, far off. I went to Sensor to confirm. I wouldn't have contacted you otherwise, but there are five objects coming our way."

"*Forget it!*"

To his dismay, Amav's shadow moved in the Sensor Room and he heard, both on the intercom and in real life five feet away: "Jack, are you there?"

"*Hell!*" He had to get down to the fuselage floor. Get to the lavatory, ignore her stupid pleas to confess all his lousy guts the way she always wanted. Sooner or later she'd get lost and Jack could sneak back up to the kitchenette and post the damn command. He'd never capitulate, never say a word, never even hear her. Okay, maybe he'd already screwed up by saying "Forget it!" out loud. It wouldn't happen again. He was just a little bit dazed by everything. Now he wondered how he'd come to be standing downstairs in front of the wreckage of the escape ship. He whirled and screamed: "*Forget it! Forget it! Forget it!*"

No response. Just the whoosh of the ventilators. Jack felt the raw female power on the catwalk above him. In fact, Amav's shadow was plainly cast on the fuselage floor, shadow hands gripping shadow catwalk guardrails.

"Dammit, Commer, you are *not* to speak to her! That's an order! You know that even the slightest attempt to speak will result in--in a *discussion* of some sort! *More* insanity! You will not, I repeat, you will *not* speak a word to her. This is an order given to you by--by Jack Commer, Supreme Commander, and--and if you disobey this order, I will find you guilty of--of treason, and you shall die by my hand, as a traitor to the USSF, and ... to *me* ..."

How could she not respond? How could she ignore *that?* How could his entire life come to such a disgraceful end? She was so ruthless, she could play the silent game so much better than he could. He'd never known how to keep his damn mouth shut. All that crap about "five mysterious objects" had been a ruse to lure him into this trap. To lure him to his *death*.

He let the ship's whirring ventilation chronicle the unraveling of his mind. Then came banging from the ventral hatch to the Pod. So now that nasty Bobby was going to ooze out of the Pod like a slug. Bobby, the precocious literary figure who knew more about how to handle women than Jack would ever know. He refused to take it. He refused to stand here and be reprimanded by a twelve-year-old boy.

"You've failed, Commer!" he hissed. "And you know what the penalty for that is." He grabbed the heat blaster at his belt. But he wouldn't draw it just yet. Let Amav savor his suicide a bit, let her cry out: *"No, no, Jack, I love you, you can't do it, I'll do anything!"*

The hatch burst open. It took Jack a long time to realize it was just Rogers and Pollard blinking at the harsh light. Pollard stumbled into Rogers.

"Watch out, jerk!" Rogers grunted, waving some sort of stick.

"Sorry, baby, this place is so damn *bright*. I can hardly see!"

"Hey, Commer!" Rogers shouted. "We wanna have a talk with you!"

Jack stared at a point over the heads of the punk ruffians. He wasn't about to have a little chat with those twits, either. How did they get into the ship against the booby trap?

"You crazy, Commer? You deaf? Whatsa matter with ya, baby?" Rogers taunted, edging around the demolished escape craft waving his stick, or rather, Jack saw, a twelve-inch kitchen knife.

"Jack! They've got *knives!*" Amav screamed from above.

Jack whirled. "Dammit, I can see that! Just *forget it!* Who said you could talk? I'm not speaking to you!"

"You damn idiot! They have *knives!* They want to kill you!"

"I told you I never wanted to speak to you! Ever again!" But Jack found himself locked into her angry deep brown eyes, into her sensuous oval face framed by lustrous long dark hair, into her breasts pushing tightly from her red flight suit as she strained against the guardrail. God, he hadn't seen any of *that* since-- since when?

"You--you--" he gasped. "You want me *dead!*"

"You damn idiot! *They* want you dead! Rogers and Pollard! Look, they're almost on you! Blast them down, for God's sake!"

"Commer! C'mon, baby! We're coming for ya!" Pollard snarled from a crouch, waving his own foot-long serrated blade.

"Forget it, they're just punks, I don't need that crap!" Jack shouted. "You just get back in the Sensor Room and shut the damn door! I'm not speaking to you!"

"Yeah, Amav honey, like he ain't talkin' ta ya," Rogers said, slashing his knife around. "*We'll* talk ta ya after we slice hubby to hamburger!"

"Keep out of this!" Jack snarled. "This is strictly a family matter!"

"You idiot! Blast them! Blast them now!" Amav screamed.

"Dammit, you're always panicking! I can't even go to the kitchen to post an order without you screwing everything up! I'm so sick of this!"

"You're a stubborn fool, you've always been a stubborn fool, why the hell did I ever marry you?"

"Why *did* you ever marry this pinhead?" Pollard said, edging forward. "He's such a wimp!"

"*We'll* marry you!" Rogers guffawed.

"Yeah! After we carve hubby up!"

"Dammit, you're all making me *talk*," Jack complained. "I said I wasn't ever going to open my goddamn mouth again, and you're all making me *talk*! I'm so sick of all this! I'm having to explain everything and I'm sick of it! Everyone's *pissing* on me and I don't know why! This whole mission has been--really bad, you know!"

"These people threaten your life, they threaten to *rape* me, and you sit there feeling sorry for yourself?" Amav yelled.

"Now you're accusing me of letting these jerks rape you! That's what makes me so sick! You're so damn unfair!"

"They're on top of you! You idiot! Kill them! Kill them!"

"I wouldn't let these twits rape you! You're my damn wife! What kind of accusation is *that?*"

"Forget it, dude, we *are* gonna rape the bitch, and she's gonna enjoy every second of it!" Pollard chortled.

"Before we slice off her tits, that is!" Rogers laughed.

Jack spun around. His idiot wife was right for once in her

life. These losers *were* right on top of him with those knives.

"Excuse me, but I'm having a private argument with my wife, and--aw, crap! There, you made me admit I'm actually talking to her!" He turned back to Amav. "*Forget it!* I'm not having an argument with you! I'm not speaking to you!"

"They'll kill you!" Amav screamed. "Jack! Jack!"

"Aw, forget it, I'm in the flow, I've got my heat blaster, these jerks can't--"

But Rogers and Pollard were flying, dropping the knives and wrestling for the heat blaster Jack was pulling out of his right holster. Jack felt his fingers pried loose. He reached for the shattergun in his left holster. It was gone.

Pollard had the shattergun. Rogers had the blaster.

"Hey, Mr. Space Pilot," Rogers said, "that was easy. Now we're gonna fry ya, ya bastard!"

Nowhere to leap, no open doors, and the ruined escape craft offered no cover. Pollard and Rogers backed out of jumping distance. Jack couldn't grab both guns at once anyway. "Okay, Amav," he ordered, "get into the Sensor Room and shut the door! I mean it!"

"No!" she screamed.

"Dammit, I'm serious! Just get in there and shut the door! Tightly!"

"You can't exile me! You can't keep exiling me! I'm your wife! You just admitted that!"

"Amav, can't you please follow one single order your commanding officer gives?"

"I'm not in the damn USSF! You can't order me around!"

"*Get in the sensor room, dammit!*"

"I'm bored, Carl," Pollard yawned. "Can we please waste the dude before he yaks us all to death?"

"I won't go!" Amav cried. "I'll watch you die if I have to! If it's the only way to be with you!"

Jack staggered back. How could any human being utter such a thing? That was his *wife* up there. She actually *said* that. "I'm *not* gonna die, dammit! Just trust me and get into the goddamn Sensor Room!"

"Jack!"

"Just get in there! I know what I'm doing!"

"Aw, piss on this! Waste the slit, Nate!" Rogers snarled. "We'll never screw her!" Pollard aimed his shattergun at the Sensor Room and fired a blue-purple beam. Jack raised his arm in a futile attempt to block the ray, and turned to see it bounce off the slammed Sensor Room door.

"Bitch ..." Pollard muttered.

"See here, Commer," Rogers said. "On the count of three, Nate, we melt this guy to warm--"

Jack pulled his left hand down and stared at it. "Your shot! Grazed my wrist! My God! I'm cracking! *Cracking!*" His eyes met Pollard's. "How could you *do* this?"

Rogers and Pollard grinned. Like Jack, they knew a shatter beam graze caused a slow-motion shatter death that could take twenty agonizing seconds to complete. Jack recalled the novel Joe had made him read last year where this guy got grazed on the ankle and went through a time dilation where the shattering seemed to take twenty years. The descriptions of the cracking of the calf, the thigh, the intestines, the lungs, each stage interwoven with meditations on the victim's life history and the growth of a monstrous philosophy of despair and pain, had been too much for even Jack Commer to stomach, Jack Commer who'd personally killed two billion human beings and blown a vast chunk of Asia to subatomic particles to end the Final War.

And now Rogers and Pollard knew they had him.

"God! Oh God!" Jack screamed, clutching his wrist.

"Yeah!" Rogers laughed. "Die, Commer, die!"

"Hey, what's the mother doing there?" Pollard said.

The next couple seconds did seem to take twenty years, but they gave Jack exactly the time he needed. "Amav! Stay inside!" he shouted as he floated to the floor, punching commands on the polished green metal of the USSF Comm strapped to his wrist below the unscathed lines of his left hand.

He finished the code for full fuselage blasting. Rogers and Pollard yelped, turning to each other with bulging eyes as the anti-personnel lasers flooded up and down the length of the ship, the coated fuselage walls reflecting the rays back and forth. Rogers and Pollard were engulfed in orange light, their hideous screams cut short as they were blasted to oily gray smoke.

Jack lay spreadeagled on the floor, head turned aside, struggling to keep his body flatter than the 8.25-inch height of the lowest bank of lasers. His hair burned and his clothes were scorching as the long seconds of terrifying laser storm ticked off. The interior temperature of the ship shot to unbearable levels.

Then it was over. There was silence. Emergency air-conditioning kicked in, venting the heat into the near-absolute zero of outer space, and Jack was finally able to take a breath. The hair on his arms was burned into stiff little curls. And his clothes were gone. The blackened remnants fell apart when he got to his knees. His whole body was red.

He felt hands on his raw shoulders. "Jack! God, are you all right?"

He looked into Amav's brown eyes. "God, Amav, I'm *sorry!* I've been the world's worst idiot!"

"Jack, you wanted me to live! You care about me!"

"Well ... well, of course," Jack whispered. "Of course ..."

"You love me! You still love me!"

"Well, yes ..." And Jack Commer, Supreme Commander, USSF, was crying.

"Jack, I love you, too! You know that!"

"Not--" He was ashamed to say it. "Not Sperry?"

"Of course not!" Amav leaned forward to kiss him. "I love you, Jack! You're my husband! You're everything to me!"

But Jack was still crying. "I know, I know ..." He tried to push her away but didn't have the strength.

"Jack, love, it's okay! Whatever happened, it's okay! We love each other! That's all that matters!"

"But I've messed it up, Amav! Everything! I'm so ashamed!"

"It's all right, it's all right! It doesn't matter what happens now!"

Before he knew it Jack was kissing her. Many times. His *wife*. His *mate*. "Oh, Amav, I really love you!"

"Jack, do you realize you don't have any clothes on?"

"Well, yes …"

"Well, I need to be that way, too." And she yanked her flight suit zipper past her navel.

His wife's perfect breasts, naked beneath that suit. Unzipped for Jack alone. How could he have forgotten them? How could he have forgotten everything about Amav?

"*Amav* …" He shivered. "Oh, *yes* …"

She wriggled out of everything and straddled him, kissing him, joining him. Her body was a balm for all the burns, for all the hurt they'd caused each other. Mostly the hurt he'd caused her, he saw.

But they were making love, they were *marrying*. They'd grow beyond the hurt. What was that concept always in the back of Dar's mind? *R'mrel'lasktm'uu?*

Then the gravity was gone. The lights went out. Amav and Jack floated. Intense new lights strobed through the *Typhoon* portholes. Clankings reverberated through the ship.

CHAPTER FOURTEEN
Clopt and Company
Saturday, March 17, 2035, 0330 hours

One of the huge Alpha Centaurian stormtroopers finished reducing the escape craft to dust as his four comrades herded their captives into the center of the *Typhoon*.

"This will make it easier to blast you all to atoms at once," he said, adjusting his pulsar tube and motioning the captives into a tighter circle. "I am Clopt. I command this mission."

Arms and legs shackled by force fields, Jack looked through Borman's turret to the bright white underside of one of the five Centaurian scout ships that had intercepted the *Typhoon*. At least the Centaurians had brought along their own airlock and attached it to the ship before forcing the *Typhoon's* rear hatch. These AC's were the dreaded Zarj, the same species the refugees had escaped from: nitrogen-oxygen breathers, vaguely humanoid with a head having two eyes, but with four arms and numerous sensory tentacles.

Jack dragged his heavy feet half a step out of the circle. "I'm the commander of this ship," he said. "I demand fair treatment of my crew." Although he only cared at this point for Amav and Bobby, Jack was going to press for every advantage he could.

Well, of course Jack cared for Joe, too. It was the first time Jack had seen his brother since his eyes went dead in the Control Room ten days ago. His last surviving brother, one of *them* now. The main thing Jack had remembered from Sperry's diary was the account of Joe having at it with those converted women. Jack realized that he'd secretly been hoping that Joe's penchant for casual seduction might be reasserting itself, might be preparing the way for a return to sanity. Or was that just delusional? God, what was it like in Joe's brain right now?

"We shall decide what is fair treatment, and we shall fry you as we please," came Clopt's shrieking Zarj, translated into English by Jack's USSF Comm, which had somehow survived the anti-personnel lasers. When the AC's were boarding Jack had briefly thought of using his comm to fire the lasers and kill everyone aboard, but at the same moment he saw one of the AC troopers aim a device at the walls of the ship, head straight for a control panel, and disable the APL system. "You are Jack Commer, Supreme Commander, USSF?" Clopt went on.

"I am," Jack said, hearing his comm fling back the answer in Zarj.

"And you command these vermin?"

Jack hesitated. "I command certain of them. Others are just passengers."

"He doesn't command!" Emory Bell cried. "He's a traitor to the AC's! Don't you recognize us? Friend! Friend! We are of the Head!"

"We realize that," Clopt said. "We also know that you are human vermin. We will enjoy killing you."

"But I'm so sorry I'm human! I'm sorry I displease you!"

Jack shook his head in disgust at the complement of refugees and *Typhoon* crew facing the Centaurians: Ben and Sheila, Emory, Anna Dorch, Catherine and Arbold Protor. Joe and Will and Lee and Patrick James. Phil Sperry. The three Martians, minds so dulled by weeks of conversion Jack could barely read them. But then there was the astonishing nude Amav. He'd watched the preadolescent Bobby stare at Amav's naked body, then switch himself off. It was the only sign of life he'd seen in the youngster since he'd come on board. Now the unconverted preteen pornographer stood apart, vacantly scanning the charred floor.

The five Zarj were seven feet tall and wore brilliant blue uniforms. Zarj were reputed to be the most merciless killers among the AC's. There was the story of the two Zarj troopers who'd stormed a four hundred-man battle cruiser and killed two hundred USSF with clubs and knives before robot probes tracked them down and vaporized them. Jack had no idea why anybody on the *Typhoon II* was still alive.

"You there, Commer," Clopt spoke, his harsh Zarj and his electronic English singing on Jack's strained nerves. "Is it customary for USSF ship's captains to prance about in the nude?"

Jack looked down. "What I prance about in is no damn business of yours."

Clopt's folds along the middle of his face contracted spasmodically. "I have orders not to kill you, or I most certainly would begin that task by death-raying those curious appendages between your legs."

Jack smirked. So these jerks didn't have the authority to hurt them. They'd be taken somewhere, maybe to some high official, maybe to the Emperor himself. Jack might just be able to talk their way out of this mess, maybe even salvage the mission.

"Sons of bitches," he muttered, just to see the effect it had. His comm was the only one among the prisoners. He'd long ago taken away those of his converted crew, and Amav hadn't been wearing hers, so everyone had to wait for the device on Jack's wrist to translate Zarj to English and English to Zarj. The comm couldn't do a thing for the dull Martian outradiance, but the Martian mental drool certainly wasn't worth paying attention to in Martian, English, or even Zarj.

Clopt raised something like an eyebrow above one of two messy purple whirlpools in his forehead. "*Guh ... llh ... seemmelll ... szeeeerrrree!*" spat the AC Commander. This came out on Jack's translator as "To the copulation of self!" Well, the comm wasn't perfect, although version 7.6 of the USSF Translator was a breakthrough in translation technology. In fact, 7.6 had been a major factor in the optimism behind the *Typhoon II* voyage. Everyone felt that some meaningful communication with the AC's could at last be achieved.

It had taken several minutes for the Zarj to adjust to the human device broadcasting back to them in decent Zarj. The troopers had seemed shocked at first, but Clopt seemed to revel in his ability to taunt his captives.

"We realize that all but three of you are already Converted to the Head," Clopt said. "I shall expect complete obedience from the Converted. And as for Commander Commer, the naked whore, and the immature human, they are expressly warned to follow our commands, because nothing in our orders forbids us from causing you pain and physical mutilation."

"That's right, Jacko," Arbold Protor spoke up. "You've met your match. Accede to the Head. It'll do you good."

"Silence!" another Zarj trooper spat, raising a tentacle with a gleaming blue tube.

"What's the trip, Protor?" Jack said. "You're the new honcho of the brainwashed, now that I've fried Pollard and Rogers?"

"Silence!" Clopt screeched.

"Do as they say," Phil Sperry whispered. "I'm on their Head Wavelength now, and they're getting *mad*."

"Aw, forget it, Sperry," Jack snarled. "You're all traitors to the human race! And take your goddamn eyes off Amav! You're never gonna have her!"

"Hey, man, ease up, man," Sperry said, raising his hands. "We're all of the Head here, or soon to be, so I say, everyone ease up, have a good time, and we'll be okay. Amav's just one more good-lookin' chick, man. No problem, you know."

"Silence!" shrieked another trooper. "Captain, shall I blow a few of them to atoms?"

"Not yet," Clopt said. "We have our orders. They are a talkative bunch, aren't they, though? Even our Converted do not know the meaning of true piety to the Head."

"They *are* vermin," the trooper agreed.

"We understand how you might feel that way," Protor said. "We're just so glad you found us! This Commer bastard is *crazy*. My God, we could've spent an eternity cruising around out here! How ever did you find us?"

Clopt made a sound like a cat hacking up a hairball. "Do you really think you were found by accident? Do you really think the Emperor could be kept in the dark about anything going on in His Empire?"

"Well … of course not!" Protor babbled. "I can't mean any offense to the Emperor! I'm of the Head, after all! It's just that, well, we did steal your ship, after all, and once our Star Drive went out, I assumed we were completely lost."

Clopt's undefined eyes wrinkled at Protor. "Our spies informed us long ago of this human ship's coming invasion. Of course we sent you straight towards this vessel."

"I don't understand, sir, I mean, sire! I mean, we're so sorry we stole that ship of yours, I mean, we know it was a sin, but we felt compelled to do so!"

"Fools! You felt compelled because we put the idea into your minds to steal it! Do you vermin really think you could have overpowered a squadron of Zarj stormtroopers on your own? We knew you were possible Seeds of Conversion, and we programmed the ship to intercept this human invader. We knew the two Star Drive fields would cancel each other out. Then you Seeds would infect the humans on this ship, and it would turn around and infect your entire solar system. But we saw our own ship was disabled and that this ship failed to head to Sol. It was easy to trace your location."

"Well, hail to the Emperor!" Protor said. "It's brilliant! I thought we were *escaping* the Zarj, coming back to infect the United System in our own way, but in reality, we were part of a Divine Plan all along! The Emperor's Divine Plan!"

"Wait, are you saying two Star Drives can cancel each other out?" Sperry cried. "Is that possible? Interacting like that? That's incredible! We've never thought to fire two ships at each other in Star Drive, but I could see--"

"Silence!" Clopt said. "Your speculation is pointless. We learned long ago that Star Drives can disable each other under certain conditions. It's enough that the Emperor has ordained this."

"Oh, yes, yes of course," Sperry muttered. "The Emperor! Of course!"

"But you could've told us everything," Protor persisted. "Such a brilliant plan! You should have taken us into your confidence!"

"Why should we inform vermin of our plans? You had to believe you were stealing a ship on your own, so that Commer here in turn would believe you," Clopt said. "However, enough talk. You will all silence yourselves now, for this conversation begins to sicken me. My comrades are also sickened. They may start killing indiscriminately."

"Aaah, you're bluffing," Jack said. "You're just a bunch of flunkies who can't hurt us, because you know as well as I that we're on a peacekeeping mission to see the Emperor. And I demand to be treated as the United System's representative with full plenipotentiary powers."

"Shut up!" Lee Borman moaned. "Jack, don't *ever* insult a Centaurian! Can't you see that they're like the radiance of--of God?"

"Ah, forget it, these are the worst low-class jerks they could afford to send. Everyone knows the AC war effort's been losing steam for quite a while now. We all know the Emperor has to make peace or lose his hold on the populace."

"Silence, absolute *silence!*" Clopt roared. "I will have no more disturbances, or I will kill you despite my orders to the contrary!"

There was brief quiet. Jack noticed that Arbold and Catherine, along with Ben and Sheila, were painfully kneeling in their force field shackles. To Jack's astonishment they, along with Anna and Emory, began to chant:

"Oh ... most holy ... Head ..."

"What the hell?" Amav said.

"We don't ... wanna be dead ..."

"It's the Ancient Chant of the Head!" Sperry whispered. "The most holy thing a Centaurian can ever utter in his lifetime! It guarantees immortality! Why have I never remembered it until now?" And he was on his knees as well.

"Feed us ... lots of nice ... bread ..."

Then Borman and Patrick James, Connors, Joe, and all three Martians were also chanting:

"Herd us ... into ... your bed ..."

The congregation lifted the last note and let it fade harmoniously. The five blue troopers stared at those kneeling. Jack was stunned. A group of human beings had just chanted five merciless Centaurian killers into silence. There was no way the troopers could interfere with the Chant. It was that powerful. In fact, the Chant was *glorious*. And why shouldn't it be? It was a force for peace, it subdued the violent, it calmed the soul, it taught the ancient wisdom. Wasn't that the whole point of this mission? Peace, wisdom, an end to war? The Chant led them all straight to Heaven!

Yes! Yes! Sperry was right! Conversion--Inclusion--makes sense! Unbelievable!

"Jack! Don't!" came the cry. Amav was at his side, shaking him as best she could with her force-field-shackled hands. "It's nonsense! The Chant is nonsense! It's all mumbo jumbo! Shake it off!"

"Amav! I--I--" He shivered. "Yes! It's nonsense! The Chant is nonsense!" He turned to Clopt. "My God! All you AC's are *brainwashed!*"

Clopt grinned, or what passed for a grin with all those vertical folds in his face. "It does keep the masses quiet," he said, pointing to those gazing stupefied at the floor. Jack had been wrong about the troopers. All five were grimly alert. "But we don't care a bit for religious chants. The Head is simply a device to marshal our energies for war, no matter what the masses might think."

"Oh, but you're wrong," Arbold Protor said, slowly rising with clasped hands, as did all the rest. "The Head is for Peace. The Emperor is for Peace. You military creatures think it all revolves around you, but the Emperor knows that once he's attained Peace, the need for military systems will dissolve."

"You think so, eh?" Clopt said.

"There is no need to treat us with sarcasm. I am your friend, after all."

"Human, we AC's have fried your brothers and sisters, thousands of them, in this war. Are you so spineless as to call us friend?"

"Sir, I believe I am courageous enough to call you friend."

Two of the troopers exchanged what could only have been a glance of disgust.

"No, we *are* your friends!" Fulr put in, forcing himself to speak English so the USSF Translator could clarify his muddy outradiance. "Read my thoughts! Flow with them, feel the love all we Converted have for you. Renounce the weapons of war.

Stop loving death and killing the way Jack Commer does. He is your enemy and ours, but does not yet realize the futility of his opposition. Soon he shall Convert. As I have Converted. Read my mind, see my soul! Oh, if only I could know yours!"

"Yes," Clopt sneered, "I have felt your weak minds leaking out from the three of you Martians from the moment I stepped in here, and I had to stop for a moment to regain control of my stomach bladder. You are all truly repulsive."

"But we love you," Dar protested. "You especially, Clopt, are the embodiment of all that is noble and courageous in the Centaurian race."

"There are many Centaurian races," Clopt shot back, "and we quarrel furiously. To speak of *one* Centaurian race is blasphemy."

"Then you must have misunderstood him," Kner put in. "Dar meant, of course, that the Zarj embody the perfection that will someday be the ruling race of the entire galaxy."

"Because we love you so," said Dar.

"Sheesh," Jack muttered. This idiocy was especially disturbing because of what Jack had known the Martian mind to be: resilient, patient, and profound. Now it was gurgling like a sick infant.

"For instance," Fulr went on, "if you only knew how badly it hurts our souls to be handcuffed by these force fields, when we can never be of any harm to you. To feel your distrust of us even though you can clearly read to the depths of our souls the love we feel for you. If you only knew how badly these force fields hurt our weak Martian hands and wrists. We beg of you, unshackle us, so that we may love you all the fuller, as divine representatives of the Emperor's very--"

"I've had enough of this BS!" a trooper snarled. "If the force fields bother you, why then, I'll cure you of that problem!" The trooper raised his pulsar tube and blasted the upper half of Fulr's body into bright blue nothingness.

Jack gaped at the bottom parts of the Martian collapsing in a charred stench next to Ben McCasland, who stood paralyzed, eyes wide, mouth twisted.

"God--damn!" Jack gasped. Unlike a human heat blaster or Martian shattergun, the pulsar tube's ray wasn't powerful enough to fully vaporize its victim. Its billions of short-lived mini-neutron stars simply tore through and absorbed what they could before the microscopic stars dissolved. Fulr's lower body twitched and was still.

"You--you can't!" Protor cried. "This is not Love! This is not the Head! You can't kill!" He turned to Clopt. "Your subordinate has defiled the Head!"

"I support my subordinates in all their decisions," Clopt said calmly, raising his pulsar tube and firing at Protor's midsection.

"Yaaa--!" Protor cried, stomach blasted away. The shot caught Emory Bell in the head, and he too collapsed, writhing in agony.

"God! No!" Anna Dorch screamed, and felt the full impact of a pulsar tube.

The rest of the captives got the message: shut up, stifle all emotion at the sight of blood and entrails, stand straight, stay in line, don't move. Jack noted that his fellow military crewmembers composed themselves faster than the civilians, who still struggled to swallow cries of horror and anguish. Jack worried about Amav, but naked and helpless, she controlled herself with chin held high. Bobby Athens stood with his eyes closed. Each of the blue-uniformed AC's calmly held his pulsar tube at the ready, oblivious to the last cries of the dying.

"Hand me that human heat blaster there," Clopt said, accepting the weapon from one of his subordinates. Jack braced for the end. Set on wide dispersion that gun could fry the remaining captives in a second. Or an hour, if Clopt chose. Instead Clopt waved the captives back and fired the blaster at the soggy debris on the floor. Before long all traces of the bodies were gone, except for the smell.

Clopt counted the remaining captives. "Thirteen of you left. How many more will it take before I have complete respect?" He let a long silence go by. "Very good. I see that even our remaining Martian friends have deigned to cease transmitting."

Dar and Kner's minds had shut down in shock and

mourning for their comrade Fulr. Jack knew the Martian ideal was to choose the time of one's own death. Fulr was probably the first Martian in eons, outside of the recent Hergs war, to die unexpectedly. It was probably for the best that Dar and Kner had closed down. They probably would've been blasted instantly for any thoughts they had.

"I want you to understand, Jack Commer," Clopt went on, "that I am not bluffing. I have allowed these four to die to demonstrate this matter to you. My orders are to transport you to the Emperor's palace aboard the Imperial Flagship near Proxima Centauri, but this need not necessarily include the rest of the captives. If I hand over just you, I will have fulfilled my mission perfectly. Even if you must be killed, I can always say you resisted captivity and had to be destroyed, and no one will fault even that. The only reason I keep any of your passengers alive is that I know I can kill them off one by one if need be to retain your attention. Is that clear?"

"Aaah, I can easily dispense with any of these converted twits anyway," Jack shot back.

"And these two Nonconverted?" Clopt said, jerking a tentacle at Amav and Bobby. "You understand, of course, that you are in fact to be granted full plenipotentiary powers in your audience with the Emperor. We'll use the fate of the Nonconverted to ensure a smooth negotiating process. Is that clear?"

Jack took a breath and hobbled in his shackles to Amav. "Okay, listen up, Clopt. This is my wife. She is not to be harmed under any circumstances. She's the most important person here. You will not harm her. Is that understood? Or there can be no thought of negotiations."

Clopt widened his eyes. "You dare declare her untouchable?" He fingered his pulsar tube.

"Jack, no!" Amav said. "Don't you dare!"

"I'm sorry, Amav, I don't care. I'm being selfish now. I don't give a damn about anything. No matter what happens, I'm not going to let them hurt you."

"But it's no use! You'll wind up signing away the entire

United System, and as soon as you do sign, we'll both be tortured to death anyway!"

Clopt grinned. "I would say that is about right."

"Forget it. It doesn't matter," Jack said. "I'll negotiate anything you want, as long as she's not hurt. I can't bear to see her hurt."

Amav regarded the ashes at her bare feet. "When the time comes, I want you to bear it, Jack. Whether or not you know it now, you'll do what's right."

"Increase force field shackles to maximum!" Clopt snapped. A trooper turned a dial on his belt. Jack's legs and arms buckled with extra gravities and his entire body became rigid.

"You will stand at attention in the hold of this putrid ship as we tow it to Proxima Centauri!" Clopt snarled, striding around the thirteen frozen figures. Jack could see only straight in front of him, part of Amav's shoulder and her hair. He couldn't meet her eyes, but he knew they were both thinking: *I love you. We're together now. We came back together.*

Nothing else mattered except that the horrible months of separation were over. And here at the end, Jack knew who he was. He wasn't the Supreme Commander of Everything, he was just a man in love, and if he had to sell the universe down the hole so Amav could live a few seconds longer, by damn he'd do it.

Clopt extended a tentacle to the top of Jack's force field. Jack felt no sensation as Clopt pulled the field forward. He simply watched his environment roll around until he came to a halt on the floor. If he could have moved a muscle, he would have smiled. Above him towered the nude form of his lover. He would spend the journey to the Emperor's palace contemplating his beautiful wife.

"Your bodies are revolting," Clopt said. "But they will not last very long in Proxima Centauri anyway."

CHAPTER FIFTEEN
Let's All Wallow in Mental Illness
Monday, March 19, 2035, 1100 hours

Thousands of dignitaries crowded the Emperor's Receiving Hall. Ship's Archivist Polot was stunned to find himself in the first row in front of the Emperor's empty dais. Like ninety-nine percent of the Emperor's Personal Retinue aboard the thirty-five-mile-long Imperial Flagship *GnlSaljPraraq,* he'd never seen the blazing green tiles and the soaring purple arches of the impossibly vast and high Receiving Hall, much less the Emperor himself. Yet as soon as the message arrived ordering him to the first row, Polot knew he'd be expected to provide in-depth information on human culture, the history of Earth's United System, and biographical material on Jack Commer, Emperor of the Humans.

When the Emperor arrived Polot would be able to recite all the relevant material in four hours.

As a Jujl, the most humanoid of Centaurian species, standing six feet, nine inches, with two arms, two legs, two eyes, a single nose and a single mouth, Polot began with a better-than-average understanding of human physiology. His extensive studies of humanity had given him a keener perspective of that species than perhaps any other Centaurian possessed.

Polot's well-known hobby, his theoretical "Time Viewer" for tracing quantum events backwards in time, was undoubtedly another major reason for his standing here today. Polot's fascination with human history had inspired the Time Viewer. For if such a Viewer could be built, one would actually be able to see past human events unfolding, and possibly answer the question of just how this strange race had evolved to become an obstacle to the expansion of the Alpha Centaurian Empire. In researching and publishing his Time Viewer to the Grid, Polot had agonizingly brushed up on several areas of study, including theoretical physics and computer programming, which he'd long ago abandoned for his career as an archivist. His final publication, "A Time Viewer for the Comprehension of Enemy

Human History," had even won praise from the famous Zarj physicist Dlatglaw, who saw no reason why such a Time Viewer couldn't succeed. "After all," Dlatglaw said, "all it would be doing would be gathering quantum information about the universe."

In truth, Polot empathized with the human species so well that when the thirteen captives were brought in, under the guard of the merciless Clopt, the Emperor's Head of Security, Polot had trouble repressing a surge of sexual desire for one of the women. Polot had no idea why the woman wore no clothing, but her body, moving slowly under the effects of force field shackles, exuded a taut grace that left Polot breathless. One of the men was also naked. He too was a marvelous physical specimen.

But Polot immediately pulled these thoughts back. Only the fact that there were thousands of Centaurian officials around him had let his thinking go undetected. As Ship's Archivist he was naturally granted a higher measure of curiosity than the average Centaurian, but it was assumed he'd only exercise such curiosity when surrounded by his research computers in the Archives sixty flights below this hall. To scan and appreciate outside the Archives would signal that Polot had wandered from the Head.

Wandering from the Head was bad enough, but to do it in the Emperor's Receiving Hall was unthinkable. It was likely the entire ceremony would be halted so that Polot could be tortured in front of everyone.

Nevertheless, the humans were beautiful. Now Polot recognized the naked man as Jack Commer, the Human Emperor. He trudged in his force shackles with his fellows down the center aisle of the Hall and was brought to a halt twenty feet from the Emperor's dais, a few yards from where Polot stood to the left of the throne.

Polot had studied the human phenomenon of "the hero" extensively. Commer definitely fit it, and so did the young woman, who had to be Amav Frankston-Commer. Polot began comparing the holographic images of the captives that had been transmitted to the Archives with the humans and Martians who stood before the dais. Before long he had all the names and bodies matched up. Polot noted Jack Commer's bright red skin and the hair burned off his head and torso. Apparently the hero Commer had tried to commit suicide by flooding his own ship with death rays rather than submit to the Head.

Polot returned to the stunning Amav. Polot had never heard of mating between the Jujl and humans, but knew it was physically possible. He was abruptly curious about it in a way he'd never dreamed. It was treason to even consider it, but this Amav had an aura about her that Polot couldn't explain. The other women there, Sheila McCasland and Catherine Protor, were merely drab. The other men appeared stunned and unintelligent. There was also a young human, what the humans termed a "boy," who was cold, expressionless, and probably mentally disturbed. The two Martians also wore no expression. Polot had heard about their ability to transmit thoughts, but so far hadn't succeeded in picking up any.

Whatever their mental state, the captives shared a similar look of illness and exhaustion, if Polot has studied his human medical manuals correctly. He'd heard that the Warp Transfer, what the humans called "Star Drive," had malfunctioned five times during Clopt's trip back to the Imperial Flagship. Clopt had blamed it on the complicated task of keeping the captured *Typhoon II* interlocked with his own Warp Transfer Field, but everyone knew how unstable Centaurian Warp Transfers were. At any rate, Polot had heard that the captives' spasms of nausea were so horrendous that Clopt had assumed they were all dying.

Yet, even pale and unsteady, Amav was lovely. So was Jack Commer. Polot was fascinated by both of them. He wondered what their sexual relationship was like. Would it be possible, he wondered, to place them in the same prison cell and set up a scanner? On the other hand, wouldn't that be an invasion of what they called their Privacy?

Privacy was an impossible concept for a Centaurian to fathom, as it involved an individual desiring separation from the whole. In Centaurian terms, it would be like telling the Emperor you didn't want to be part of the Head. Yet the more Polot studied this concept of Privacy, the more intrigued he was by it. Not only did Privacy mean that the process of thinking was carried out in entirely different ways than in the Centaurian mind, but it also meant that human beings could experience "emotions," surges of staggering psychic energies created at a moment's notice, all of which were hidden from other individuals.

Centaurians knew nothing of such states. Their minds were carefully regulated by the Head, or to be more precise, the Grid of Mental Energies that radiated from the Emperor, through his highest to lowest advisors, and then on out into the cognitive bureaucracy in which every Centaurian had a position and duties.

Even the Martians, so Polot understood, had developed a form of Privacy despite their ability to read each other's minds. Apparently, since Martian telepathy was based on the ability to *project* thoughts, rather than passively read them, the emphasis was on volitional broadcasting of the inner psyche, rather than being part of an obligatory Grid.

So Polot wished to respect this concept of Privacy. Unlike the rest of the Centaurians here today, he did not clamor for the captives to be brain-scanned by electrofield machines and the results dropped into the computers in the Archives. He had a feeling that the brain scans would reveal nothing anyway.

Eight of the humans, and the two Martians, had Converted, but Polot knew these ten were by no means fully integrated into the Head. They were still too feeble to participate in the Grid, to hold positions and execute duties. They were still in the intoxicated stage of feeling at one with an entity greater than themselves. Let them discover ultimately what a chore it was to participate fully in the Head.

But again Polot had to watch himself. Weren't these treasonable thoughts? Wasn't he himself beginning to engage in Private concepts he didn't wish to feed into the Grid of the Head? Things the Emperor must not know? What a queer sensation. Exhilarating, like the way he felt when he looked at that Amav creature.

How could these humans and Martians ever fully Convert? Wasn't there, at the core of these races, a need for Privacy that would ultimately reassert itself? Or was it to be called dignity? Weren't these Converted merely enjoying a big drunk right now? Wouldn't they sober up soon?

Could Polot be destined to play a major part in the sobering, not only of these Converted, but of the Centaurian Elite itself? His heart surged with the thought. For if he could adequately express his deep perspective on human psychology, wouldn't humans and Centaurians see they were simply leading two separate sorts of existences, Privacy and Grid? That both had their advantages? That there was no need for them to war with each other? If he could just talk with the Emperor, wouldn't Polot be able to assure the dignity of these humans, and perhaps introduce this intriguing concept of Privacy to his fellow Centaurians?

Now Jack Commer barked: "Okay, which one of you bastards is the Emperor? Let's get down to business." Instantly a squad of the Emperor's giant thin Tarl bodyguards surrounded the thirteen captives with raised pulsar tubes. Polot was transfixed by the timbre of Jack Commer's voice. He could understand the English without recourse to the thousands of small spherical translation speakers floating five feet above them all. These spheres, normally used to conduct business between the various AC subspecies, had been upgraded yesterday after Jack Commer's personal translation device had been reverse-engineered. The spheres now seamlessly translated human English to all AC languages and vice-versa.

Glarzj, also of the Tarl species, the Imperial Manager and the Emperor's chief of staff, stood in front of the blazing yellow throne, his long hammerhead skull bobbing furiously. "The Emperor is in meditation and will not arrive until he has finished." His brown-scaled arm indicated the empty throne. "Meanwhile, any show of impatience on the part of our captives will be rewarded with slow death."

"Aaah, screw it," Jack muttered.

More pulsar tubes came up, this time ringing Jack's head.

"*What* did you say?" Glarzj demanded.

"He--he said: 'I blew it,'" Joe Commer put in. "He's sorry for his outburst! That's what he means, he's my brother and I know he doesn't mean any harm!"

"Forget it, Joe," Jack said in disgust. "This is the first time you've dared to open your trap in front of me since you converted. Your mind is *gone*. It makes me sick." He turned back to Glarzj. "And I *am* impatient, you jerk. We've been held in these force shackles for two days with no food and damn little water."

"Silence!"

"I demand to be heard in my capacity as chief plenipotentiary negotiator for the United System!"

"You--" Glarzj began, motioning for a Tarl trooper to pulsar Jack's head off, then catching himself and canceling the hand signal. Polot knew no one was ready to kill the human Emperor. "Jack Commer, do not try our patience. You are here to sign the peace accords that will end the war between our empires. The accords will be presented by the Emperor. You will sign them without uttering a word."

"In return for what? Not being tortured quite as slowly as everyone else? Is that it?"

Glarzj again strained to avoid giving the death signal. Finally he turned and walked away. The entire audience murmured at Jack's irreverence. "Fry the *slursing* son of a *pliss!*" one Centaurian noble snarled, using obscenities that made Polot wince.

"*Fluzz* the *bleel!*" another noble shouted.

"*Cuckj! Clus! Schlarshz! Scaddiz-klun!*" a Fkuuh woman cried. Polot cast his eyes to the green tile. The Fkuuh were the crudest sort of barbarians. Polot was embarrassed that they were part of the Empire.

Jack Commer, having heard these last remarks through the translation spheres, simply turned to his accusers and made an odd gesture that Polot would have to look up later in the Archives: the back of the right hand with the middle finger raised. Could this lone finger possibly mean the One Oversoul?

Was Jack mollifying the barbarian shouters with an exhortation that all beings were part of One Oversoul? Polot impulsively raised his right hand and extended the middle of his three twelve-inch-long fingers to Jack, even as the shouting went on: "*Scuck! Ruddzza-scuck! Karnblurf flazzsz! Flucgk! Murgsniss!*" Polot knew the boors around him had no idea he was responding to Jack's offer of friendship. Would Jack take Polot's return gesture as proof that at least some Centaurians wanted real understanding between the empires?

Jack was evidently confused by all the snarling. He blinked at Polot's twelve-inch finger and shrugged, then looked back towards Glarzj, who returned with a squad of Tarl hoisting a velvet box on their shoulders.

As the noise dropped off Glarzj said: "It is customary to torture enemies of the Emperor at the moment they commit their crimes. And the Emperor would enjoy seeing your body slowly ripped to shreds by Radwaste Burrowers. So you had better be silent as the Emperor approaches."

"Radwaste Burrowers?" Jack muttered.

Oh no! Polot thought. *Not the Radwaste Burrowers!*

"That's right," Glarzj said. "Radwaste Burrowers. Small, slimy wormlike creatures bred to live in the reactor pits and which, once set upon your body--"

"I get the picture, man," Jack said. "Sheesh."

The Emperor was approaching. Polot would finally see him. Even now he felt the Power of the Head increasing. But he was puzzled. The four Tarl troopers carried only a velvet box. Where was the Emperor? Was this a special throne?

And yet the Centaurian Imperial Orchestra blasted the first strains of "Oh Most Holy Head," and everyone was kneeling. The guards had to belt the prisoners to their knees. The Tarl troopers mounted the golden steps of the dais and fitted the purple box into a notch in the yellow throne. They attached hoses and wires.

Polot was frightened. Those vast windows behind the throne, and the cold interstellar blackness beyond, called up the Memory. How was it possible that black windows could call up the Memory? The childhood nightmare? That cruel nightfall on the planet of his birthing? Hadn't the Grid itself absorbed the Memory? How could it reappear now when he needed all his wits?

They'd left him to fend for himself. *On the bare ground.*

His tenders had left him there for just a minute, so he was later told, so they could gather solar panels before a coming thunderstorm. But it had seemed like weeks trapped out on the open dirt. On that dark heavy world. Polot couldn't even remember the name of the planet. God, to be confined to a world, trapped on the ground, *alone.*

Polot had shrieked for his tenders to kill him on the spot.

Alone. The worst nightmare for any Centaurian. No wonder they'd embarked into the infinite spaceship colonies, no wonder they'd forged the Bureaucracy of the Grid.

Yet even as a child Polot had been confronted with the choice: to hang on, to continue existence, to risk insanity by accepting the abandonment and the exposure in the open, or to short-circuit and end it all. Centaurians could do that. Could commit suicide by desiring it. They all had a central switch flickable to either ON or OFF. Polot had chosen the ON switch at the price of his sanity. He'd thrashed in the dark wind, screaming hysterically into the thunderheads building into sunset castles of doom. And he continued to exist.

This same giddy terror was everywhere in the Receiving Hall. Where was the Emperor? The source of the Wisdom of the Grid? *What the hell was that box doing there?*

The faces of those standing near betrayed obvious panic. Most of these nobles and functionaries, like Polot, were seeing the Emperor for the first time. Others had been in previous attendance, but their demeanor, though more controlled, appeared no less disquieted.

At a signal from Glarzj the audience rose. Now Polot could see through the glass cover of the box. *The Emperor was a Scihk.* One of the revolting crab monsters from the Alpha X water world. Polot could feel the entire audience gag. That entire planet had been declared a forbidden Zone of Psychosis after the

Chemical Wars seven centuries ago.

A woman next to Polot made the mistake of gasping: "Oh, *flidpzxbck,* what a pile of *scluzzk!*"

A Tarl guard instantly hauled her out of line and pulsar-tubed her head off. She collapsed to the green tile, which, interacting with a damaged organic being, secreted noxious chemicals that turned the rest of the woman's body into twisted strands of blue gas.

Everyone pretended not to notice. Polot met the gaping eyes of Jack Commer. Then Jack, then everyone, turned back to … the Emperor. The Crab Emperor.

But the Emperor wasn't a real Scihk Crab. He couldn't be. The Crabs were five feet wide and stood four feet high on their six legs. This one looked like a Crab that had been cut up with a laser and shoved haphazardly into the purple box. Except that the creature was alive. Its yellow-orange legs writhed and thumped in that enclosed space, blood gushing through the moist tissue of scores of disconnected body parts. Every motion contradicted another. Nothing fit together. At times the creature seemed to be on the verge of thrashing right through the glass and flopping in pieces all over the floor.

One of the prisoners threw up. Two guards were on the woman Polot recognized as Sheila McCasland. Pulsar tubes appeared and flashed. Even as she hit the tile, two-thirds of her blasted to nothingness, Sheila looked more complete, more at harmony, than the Emperor could ever possibly hope to be. She turned to blue gas.

CHAPTER SIXTEEN
The Grid

"Goddammit, stop wasting these people! I don't care if they've converted or not!" Jack shouted.

Four pulsar tubes reappeared at Jack's neck, but Glarzj waved them away. "Emperor Commer, you will take one step forward and remain silent."

"I'm not the damn Emperor," Jack grunted, struggling forward five steps instead of one. "I've told you that a hundred times."

"I will have Amav Frankston-Commer radwaste-burrowed if you say another word! Is that clear, you--you *plissing schluckbleel?*"

Jack shut up. He cast an anxious look at Amav.

"Interesting!" croaked the Crab Emperor. "Emperor Commer has already communicated his desire for special protection for this thing he terms a *wife.* We find this desire amusing."

Polot was afraid he would throw up himself. These flatulent sounds issued from numerous holes emerging, soft and wet, in the surface of the writhing mass of guts. The crab legs thumped all the harder into the sides of the box. Was the Crab Emperor really tearing himself apart? Polot waited for the creature's frenzy to kill him, but in some perverted way, mocking Polot's childhood choice to *continue,* the Emperor chose not to expire, but to glory in his wriggling, mutilated guts. Gore welled from the center of the crab and the writhing became even more furious. Polot stared in shocked disgust. So did everyone else, even the guards, too awestruck to pulsar the scores of Centaurians behaving so indecently in the Emperor's presence.

Fresh blood spurted against the glass, obscuring the whirling legs and viscera. The box shook madly on the throne. The Converted tried their best to behave like loyal disciples of the Head, but their throats bobbed and their cheeks squirmed. Bobby was shut down. Amav struggled up to Jack in her shackles. The two nude humans stood ten feet from the Emperor, a contrast in beauty and wholeness to his chopped horror, and not a single guard tried to stop them.

Glarzj stood to one side observing everything, and caught Polot's eye. A Head Transmission occurred. Polot understood that his brain patterns were being monitored by the Grid. Revulsion at the Sight of the Emperor was punishable by death, and while no charge was now being made, Polot's mind would be closely studied in the future. The contact ceased, but Polot couldn't control himself. He desperately wished for the fierce independence Jack and Amav now displayed. They had Privacy. They could look at the Emperor with the disgust he deserved and no one could pry into their minds.

"Look behind the throne!" the Emperor commanded. Instantly one of the huge windows to the stars turned white, and an eighteen-foot-high representation of Amav, naked as she was now, appeared there.

"What the hell?" Jack cried.

"This computer program demonstrates how we can inflict the highest degree of torture on Amav Frankston-Commer. According to our program, we can inflict 25,134 tortures upon her body and her mind over a period of 35.9 days before she must die. The final four days will be at maximum human pain threshold level, although she will wish she hadn't been born at Pain Level Five, which will last for twelve days in the middle of the torture." As the Emperor spoke, the color graphic of Amav depicted skin being ripped off, burns applied, punctures made, limbs, genitals, and eyes being removed. "Of course, we speed up the action now to give you a better idea."

Amav Frankston-Commer stared grimly at the display. Jack swallowed and turned away. "Okay!" he snarled. "Hand me the stupid treaty and I'll sign it! But she goes free! You are not to harm her!"

"Bring the treaty forward," the Emperor commanded. "Have the Amav woman taken to her cell in preparation for being, ah, *set free*. Have the other prisoners destroyed. Jack Commer will now sign." Glarzj wheeled in a table with a metal slab atop it, upon which read, in the symbols of Centaurian

Standard next to an English translation: "WE HEREBY SURRENDER ..."

But Amav Frankston-Commer hopped forward in her shackles, yanked the slab off the table, and flung it at the Emperor's box, where it knocked a hose loose and gouged the velvet. "Forget it! I'm sick of your idiotic nonsense! I refuse to be a pawn in this craziness!"

One guard rushed to reconnect the hose. Another ran at Amav with pulsar tube blazing at maximum. Polot understood she was counting on being shot down and removing any chance of being used to make Jack surrender.

But Amav's momentum had toppled her. The blast passed overhead and caught the guard reconnecting the hose, peeling off his shoulders and neck and setting the velvet side of the Emperor's box afire. The guard staggered back with a gurgling scream, collapsed on the green tile, and turned to blue gas.

Two more guards ran to the box and extinguished the fire. Glarzj shouted: "The soldier who fired that shot in the vicinity of the Emperor's box shall put himself to death immediately!"

"Y-yes, m'lord!" this guard said, then used his pulsar tube to turn himself into a headless corpse, rising off the tile as blue gas.

"As for the guard who screamed," Glarzj went on, "his death was cowardly. I hereby declare that his entire family shall be put to death." He looked down at Amav. "That was idiotic, whore. You will really be tortured now!"

"Excuse me," the Emperor said. "Glarzj, you have not even inquired about my health, despite the fact that my sulfur line was momentarily cut off and my box was on fire."

"Ah ... sire, I did not mean to omit inquiry as to your health. I saw that you were fine, and, ah, other matters very briefly required my attention."

"Guards, kill Glarzj immediately. Also exterminate every member of his clan on Level 634."

The pulsar rays shot out. "*Yaaaaaa!*" Glarzj screamed, then toppled to the floor, billowing up as gas.

"Man, these guys don't fool around," Jack said. "And all

this blue gas smells like *scuck*."

The Emperor's entire body exploded against his bloodstained glass. "Commer!" he rasped. "Do you wish to have me begin the Amav Torture Program?"

"Forget trying to save me, Jack!" Amav cried. "They'll kill me anyway!"

"We will," the Emperor agreed. "But I could guarantee a fairly quick death."

You--you monster! Polot flashed. *Why don't you just go ahead and explode? I'm so ashamed to be part of this insane Grid!*

Polot flinched. He'd just sent this message over the Grid.

The Centaurian Penal Code computers would instantly flag it. Polot braced for one of the guards to jerk him from the front line.

He closed his eyes. But nothing happened.

"Will you sign the treaty or not?" the Emperor demanded. "Guard, replace the treaty on its stand and give Emperor Commer the Metal Burn Stylus so that he may affix his signature as United System Plenipotentiary."

"Aaah, screw it!" Jack said. "I've seen through your game. I'm not gonna sign!"

"Even if I torture Amav?"

Jack considered. "I'll die smashing my fists through your little glass case and scattering your revolting little body every which way. I'll never see her die. I can't take responsibility for her death, I suppose."

"Jack! You realized it!" Amav cried. "I love you, I really love you!"

"I just realized that I can't go against my principles, Amav. If I did, I wouldn't be myself anymore, just a quavering blob like this pile of crap on the throne. And then how could I love you? And what would be left for you to love?"

"Exactly! Jack, I can handle their stupid computer program! So can you! We're in love! We won't submit to anything!"

Yes. Being Private means that love is possible.

The Centaurians had never known love, only the Grid. No

wonder the advancing thunderstorm would terrify a Centaurian child raised to feel insane, to seek death until it was plugged back into the all-succoring Grid. Back into the infinite transcendent Head.

Yet at the top of the Head was this hemorrhaging Emperor.

The Emperor was *insane*. The Centaurian Empire was *insane*. And Polot was thinking these thoughts at full strength but no one stepped forward to kill him.

He saw why. He had somehow walled part of himself from the Grid. He was Private.

He was stunned. His thoughts weren't being channeled into the Head. Yet part of him was still feeding the standard "I'm here, I'm part of the pattern" which the Grid recognized as the mental frequency of a good citizen of the Empire. He was safe. He was the first Centaurian to ever separate from the Grid.

And didn't it logically follow that Polot would use this knowledge to join the humans and overthrow the Empire?

How could this have happened? It had to be that childhood memory of choosing life, no matter how intolerable it appeared, hanging on in the windy night on the dirt. His tenders had been astonished that he hadn't died. They'd consciously sacrificed the child, flinging it down to salvage the solar panels upon which life on that awful planet depended. They'd expected the child to choose death when abandoned, but somehow it clung to life. Deep in Polot's past the seeds of life had been planted.

"I will torture every single human here!" the Emperor screamed. "I will torture Amav next to last! Then I will torture you last! You will know, viscerally, the true meaning of pain!"

"I don't give a *scaddiz-klun schluckbleel* what you do!" Jack shot back. "As for these brainwashed jerks behind me, I don't care what happens. They've thrown in with you anyway. They're ruined."

"Not Bobby!" Amav said.

"I didn't mean Bobby. But he's obviously insane." The boy, Polot saw, was glaze-eyed. He'd shut all the death out. His Privacy had turned to stone.

But Polot was free. And he would destroy the Grid.

"Well, here is my final sentence," the Emperor said. "I grow tired of these games. Your signature is hereby forged on the treaty anyway. Our Warp Transfer systems are being upgraded to be able to mount a full-scale invasion of your solar system within a year so as to be able to enforce the treaty. Meanwhile, because we see that you wish the Converted to die, why then, they shall live. We shall put them back on the *Typhoon II* for a sublight journey back to Sol. This journey will take them twenty-one and a half years. Bobby's insanity will worsen from having to grow up among the wretchedness of the insane Converted, in a cramped spaceship, for over twenty-one years.

"As for you, Emperor Commer and your whore, I hereby sentence you both to the Maximum Centaurian Torture."

The audience gasped. Polot reeled with the cruelty of it all. He almost lost his grip on his new Privacy. But he vowed to hold to it no matter what.

"The Maximum Centaurian Torture will take place immediately. Compared to it, the physical pain of our 35.9-day torture program is nothing. Jack Commer, as you suffer the Maximum Centaurian Torture you will know that Amav is suffering the exact same agony, and it will increase your own pain. You speak bravely now, yet once the torture begins you will hate yourself for your words of bravado. Guards, take them away to their respective fates. This audience is over."

The Centaurian nobility spilled inward in the traditional Greeting of Hatred for Enemies of the Empire, pressing around the harried guards who struggled to keep distance between the humans and the snarling Centaurians.

"Dirty *slucks! Gnassid pleewagger! Kashpisz slotterblaggen! Snuz! Shif! Claz!*" came the cries.

Polot pressed forward. Patrick James said: "Well, sorry you and Amav have to die, Jack, but you know, you both really did have a chance to Convert."

"Cheer up, Jack," Will Connors said. "Death really isn't so bad. Physical pain isn't either. I've been there a bit, I guess, like the time I was hit with that laser over Altrouda. But you and Amav take care now, hear?"

"Bye, Jack," said Ben McCasland. "I know what it's like. Why, Sheila just died here a little while ago, and, well, it's tough. I know. Good luck."

"See ya around!" called Lee Borman.

"Hey, Jack, guess it's Goodbye City and all," said Joe Commer, offering a handshake which the guards shoved aside. "You've been a decent brother, y'know. We had some good times together. Sorry you didn't Convert in time. Bye! Bye, Amav!"

"*Bye* …" Jack said, stunned. "Amav, that's my own *brother!*"

"*Slif-cuck! Snatck-fagger! Golld-karpathugiss! Snurggit! Snafliss! Snuxfarp!*"

A pulsar tube blared, and a noble who'd managed to swat Bobby Athens disappeared into meat and smoke.

"Keep back! Keep back!" the guards shouted, though they were enjoying the Hatred as much as anyone.

"Jack!" Polot called in English, not caring who heard. "Some of us desired peace! And some of us desired sanity! And I will crush this madness despite all obstacles!"

Jack stared back in a daze. It was perhaps sinking in that he and his wife were about to be exterminated.

"I am the Seed! I am the Seed!" Polot cried as the guards swept the captives from the Emperor's Receiving Hall.

CHAPTER SEVENTEEN
The Execution
Monday, March 19, 2035, 1530 hours

Jack woke in the darkness, eyes aching where the Centaurian stormtroopers had beat him with the long black bars, whacking him into that tiny box.

That capsule in the Imperial Flagship cargo room had looked to be eight feet long and two wide. Jack had to be inside the thing now. His shoulders were brutally pinned against the walls. His knees, his feet, and hands were immobile. His back was jammed through a curve so tight he felt his backbone would snap. Taking a breath was painful. Well, at least there was air.

Well, of course they'd supply him with air, otherwise he'd die within a couple minutes and so no more torture fun for the Centaurians. Yes, his own torture. He wasn't going to make it this time. All those adventures, all those dangers he'd made it through, all that was over. And more from the terror of the physical inability to move, of feeling shut in a coffin, Jack was abruptly out of his mind with panic. He began screaming, but, unable to move his chest, could only issue a faint wail. The aliens, no doubt monitoring him, had to be laughing, and it further increased his panic. And where was Amav? Was she in a box now, undergoing this same horror?

The capsule lurched as if a giant sledgehammer had whapped it in the rear. "No!" Jack shrieked. It was all pain, mindless pain, the final humiliation and despoiling of self. "No! No! No!"

Jack heard a hissing and felt the capsule rolling about its longitudinal axis. Thrusters. Somehow the familiar spaceship motion calmed him. Although no part of his body could possibly float free, he recognized the internal feelings of weightlessness. Above his nose was a tiny window. He had to jam his eyes to the tops of their sockets to look out. Stars. He'd been dropped out of the Imperial Flagship.

Another hiss. The rolling sensation stopped and the capsule's nose pointed down. A blinding planet lay below, the curve of its horizon so shallow that he had to be no more than a few hundred miles above the surface. Yellow clouds cast stark shadows on an ochre landscape. Mountains, dried rivers. Craters. Jack tried to remember if there was any planet like this one in the Alpha Centauri system. He had no idea how long he'd been unconscious. He could easily have been drugged and shipped through Star Drive to any remote planet the Centaurians wished. But why?

And where was Amav?

He was in a capsule with thrusters that controlled roll, pitch, and yaw. What was it all for? Where was the torture? Was this happening to Amav? He'd never seen her forced into a capsule. But the Emperor had said they'd both get the Maximum Centaurian Torture. Didn't that mean they had to undergo the same thing? Or were there different ways the Torture could be imposed?

The horizon got flatter and flatter. This was no orbit. He'd been fired like a bullet at the surface of this planet. Jack was coming down. This was it, they were going to burn him alive. Now he'd never know what become of Amav.

He couldn't believe it could all come down to this. Something supposedly designed to drive him mad with fear, and yet, he thought, so pedestrian. Was this all they could come up with? Burning him alive?

Jack was buffeted by the first hint of an atmosphere. Well, it would get hot. But when the moment came, it would be over instantly. No more Jack Commer.

But he'd given it his best shot. His whole life. The *Typhoon* project, the migration to Mars, being Supreme Commander and trying to end this crazy war. Maybe he'd screwed a lot of it up, but, dammit, he'd given it his best shot.

Streaks of fire appeared around the edges of the window. Jack stared grimly at the patterns, expecting the craft to tumble out of control. But he became aware of the sounds of thrusters all around the ship keeping the capsule stabilized, nose pointing forward despite the atmospheric battering. Complex sensors and computers, keeping him stabilized. Why bother to stabilize a hurtling meteor? He'd burn at the same rate either way.

The capsule got hotter. Jack could barely breathe. The walls began to glow. But in a way, this wasn't so bad. He strained to focus on the patterns of orange and yellow from the front of the craft. Any second now.

His body snapped forward. Jack almost threw up at the hard deceleration. When he looked up, the flames were gone and the window showed craters and dunes and rocks hurtling a few feet beneath him at what seemed to be several thousand miles per hour.

A red sun blazed in front of him. A jagged ridge appeared on the horizon and the capsule was instantly on top of it, clearing it by three feet. The ship shot lower, and the capsule's roll thrusters activated, putting the ship into a fast spin that sent the oncoming desert landscape rotating wildly around him. Jack gasped, rushing down the blurry tunnel towards the giant red sun.

The spinning bullet plowed into the planet.

*

He came to hanging upside down. Every component of his body had to be smashed. Why was he still alive? The capsule must have flipped at the end, for out the tiny window he could see the immense ditch it had dug on the way in, stretching for miles, mounds of sand and rock piled to either side.

Now Jack understood. The ship had been programmed not to burn up. The deceleration had slowed him just enough to enable the crash landing. The Centaurians wanted him here.

But he was trapped in the capsule. And though he was too numb to feel pain, he knew it would be coming. So this was the full AC torture, he thought in disgust, to land on this planet and die pinned inside this tiny smashed spaceship. Jack wondered whether he'd suffocate, starve to death, or succumb to internal injuries first.

Okay, so trap me in here, jerks! Make me starve or whatever. Big deal! It doesn't affect what my life has meant to me one whit.

The craft cracked open and Jack tumbled out onto the hot sand.

*

Hours later, as the giant red sun settled towards the horizon and Jack could finally move his arms and legs, it hit him. He lay on the sand and laughed.

For a Centaurian, the worst fate imaginable was to be stranded alone on a planet. For one thing, the Centaurians passionately hated planetary bodies and their gravitational fields. Secondly, they dreaded being physically alone. Though they had their Head connection to their nasty Emperor, they still sought comfort from being around other Centaurians, usually in crowds of at least fifty.

The Centaurians had hoped to break Jack's mind by sentencing him to fend for himself on a hostile planet. They didn't realize this would be a death of dignity for Jack Commer. He would die in an exultation of solitude.

The same must have happened to Amav. Left to die on her own alien world. Jack wanted to blot the thought from his mind. But he also took strength from the thought of her dying with the same dignity he would. They were both strong and independent people, and they'd both make good use of these last days of their lives. They would think of each other. They both had to be realizing this about now. Jack was happy. He and his wife would, in some sense, die together.

He got to his knees. He couldn't believe that he was only bruised. Nothing was broken. After a long time he managed to stand.

The sunset was lurid and scary, but Jack loved this planet. The huge red sun had slipped halfway beneath a mountain range in the distance, and the daytime heat gave way to cool breezes. The atmosphere and its clouds were a thousand shades of purple, blue, and orange. Behind him the eastern horizon was full of stars. Jack wondered which one Amav circled, on which planet.

The rocks cast purplish shadows. As the sun sank lower, the outcroppings took on uncanny shapes, powerful volumes. Wind whistled around the rocks. Without knowing why, he turned his back to the sun and walked to the east.

*

Tuesday, March 20, 2035, 1600 hours

The chilly darkness seemed to go on forever. Even by his imprecise estimates dawn should have come hours ago. Jack was close to panicking that something had happened to the sun, that maybe the deranged Centaurians had wiped out that sun just to mess with his mind, when he realized he had no way of knowing the diameter of this planet or how many hours it took to rotate on its axis. Several hours after that insight calmed him, the sky brightened and the rim of the red giant popped up over the flat black horizon directly in front of him.

Well, at least he'd been going more or less east all night. But, exhausted and weakened by the cold, he worried that if this planet's night was really something like twenty hours long, a twenty-hour day in the open might finish him off. He was hungry and thirsty, and in his mystical zeal to wander east he'd lost the capsule, which might at least have offered some means of survival. He slowed to a shuffle. Despite his earlier boasts about a solitary dignified death, he was ready to cry at the thought of his life being wasted like this. Amav was coming to a similar end. He tried not to picture her dying, but that image broke to the surface and brought him to a stop.

Okay, so this was it. He wouldn't whine or complain. He could damn well just stop muttering all these stupid little descriptions of his death and hers. All he had to do was just fall down on the sand here and go to sleep forever. Just fall down.

I told you to fall down!

For some reason Jack's body wouldn't obey the command to die. He angrily kicked at a rock, but it gave way too easily. In fact it was soft and squishy and it cried: "*Arr--rack!*"

"Oh my God!" A small animal the size of a shoebox lay on

its back, twelve legs twitching in the air. It was covered with thin translucent pearl-colored scales glowing with a rainbow of colors. It had a head with three eyes and a mouth, and a long tail.

Without thinking Jack sank to his knees and grabbed the animal. Without being sure it was dead he bit into its neck. God, it tasted wonderful. Jack spit out the pearly scales and ate the cool, light, salty flesh. Then he bit into a vein and to his surprise the animal started gushing fresh water. Jack drank it down. The entire back of the animal was a huge slab of nourishing flesh and pure water. Jack regarded the carcass in his hands. If he could just find a few more of these things, he'd be in fine shape.

He raised his head. Hundreds of the water/flesh creatures ringed him, eying him curiously. One of them looked back and forth between Jack and the dead beast and said: *"Rack?"*

The creature trotted up on its twelve legs, and to Jack's astonishment flopped on the ground, dead. Jack shrugged in embarrassment at the hundreds of animals watching what he intended to do with their brother. "Well, sorry, guys, but … I'm just so hungry!" he gasped, grabbing the dead animal and devouring it.

"Rack? Rack? Rack? Rack?" came the chorus around him.

Another Rack ambled up and died. Jack seized it. The process was repeated again and again, an animal bleating *"Rack?"* and dying six inches from his hand. Jack had the eerie feeling that the Racks offered themselves because they knew he needed sustenance. Finally he had to shove them away. He stood up, full of energy, as hundreds of Racks scurried in all directions.

Without knowing why he ran at full speed over the rills and rocks. The Rack meat and water seemed to expand within him, burning more and more transcendent fuel, nourishing every cell of his body, enabling him to run faster and harder.

*

Wednesday, March 21, 2035, 0300 hours

A ruined temple. The remnants of a lost civilization. It looked like something out of ancient Greece with its columns and blocks, its levels sloping into a vast amphitheater. All was covered with sand, weather-beaten and crumbled. Was he hallucinating? Was the rack food some sort of drug? What if he were poisoned? But how else could he have run for what seemed like half a day? For all those hours? He had to put those thoughts out of mind. It didn't do any good to doubt what he was perceiving.

The thought of the Racks made him thirsty. At once two of the creatures ran from behind a column and plopped dead at his feet. He took them up, peeled off their neck scales, and drank their water blood. Two were all that were needed. Was the first appearance of hundreds of creatures their way of reassuring the stranger that infinite sustenance was available? In the future, would only the exact number of Racks needed appear?

The Racks … the water creatures …

Bobby! Bobby's story! The Billy character survived by eating water creatures! They had water instead of blood!

Billy had found a temple. He'd crashed on an alien planet and had to survive. He'd discovered a long-dead civilization. He'd found the Racks which enabled him to live.

It was all the same. How could this be happening? Was Jack just hallucinating?

Well, not everything was the same. Jack wasn't wearing a shiny black bio-filter suit. He was directly breathing the air of this planet. There weren't any deadly bacteria here.

Not unless he counted all the crappy negative thoughts of his life, the way he'd treated Amav the last few months, the way he'd alienated everyone, the way he'd let Jack Commer, Supreme Commander, warp his soul. Yeah, all that was definitely like a bacteriological war that would wipe out a whole planet.

Well, that was all certainly poetic, but it didn't do him a damn bit of good. Jack reached for the EnviroField generators that had to be keeping him alive in this alien environment. But he patted bare stomach. He looked down. Throughout the day and a half he'd been on this planet he hadn't been wearing a thing.

Well, that took care of worrying about heat and cold. If he could survive this easily in the open with no clothes, he had to be in a pretty temperate climate.

His nude body reminded him of Amav's nude body. Maybe on her own planet she was discovering right this instant that she was as naked as he was.

No. It couldn't be. Could it? Could Bobby's story really be true? Hadn't Bobby written that "Angela" was on the other side of the planet?

"Angela" is Amav! She has to be here! On this planet!

And Amav had said she'd read all of Bobby's stories, so she had to know that the Billy character walked east and the Angela character walked west until they met.

Jack laughed. The Emperor and Empress had arrived to take charge of their empire.

CHAPTER EIGHTEEN
The Radiators
Monday, April 9, 2035, 2130 hours

"Dar! Dar!" Sperry was yammering.

"Aw, c'mon, man, knock it off up there," Joe muttered, sprawled on his mattress on the floor of the *Typhoon* fuselage. "You're interferin' with the Peace of the Head, fer gawdsake." For the past week he'd taken to sleeping in the *Typhoon* proper, on the floor. He was acting Captain, of course. Not that anybody listened to him. Like Sperry up there, babbling at the haggard Martian on the catwalk in front of the Sensor Room.

Someone had to run the show. Someone had to lie here on the mattress and be in charge. "You two just get on back into the Pod," Joe drawled. "You're disturbin' my damn Concentrated Head."

"No, it's *weird,* Joe! I've finally been able to get some of Dar's thoughts!" Sperry said, moving to Dar who stared forlornly at the blast marks on the fuselage floor where the hapless Fulr had been pulsar-tubed.

"Yeah, and so damn what?"

"Yes, so what," Dar mumbled. "It doesn't matter. I apologize for leaking my unworthy mind."

"But, Dar," Sperry's voice echoed harshly through the fuselage, "that means you're beginning to transmit thoughts again. I can catch a few of 'em right now!"

"Hey, forget it! That's an order!" Joe called up. "Sperry, I thought I told you to figure out the lock on that damn hatch." He pointed to the Control Room which had been locked against them for three weeks. "Can't be a goddamn captain if I can't fly the goddamn ship."

Sperry shrugged. "Been working on it in my spare time, man. But hey, the ship's on autopilot anyway. Nothing we need to do, you know." He turned back to Dar. "I'm really feeling your thoughts streaming out again! After all this time of blankness!"

"But it doesn't matter," Dar said. "Fulr is dead. I still can't

161

understand why the soldiers of our Beloved Emperor would kill him."

"Look, I can understand what you're saying, Dar, but you know, this is hard to say, but I'm also getting some thoughts out of you, that, well, sound pretty angry at those guards for killing Fulr."

"Well … I suppose you could say that."

"And I'm also getting the impression that you're angry with the Emperor for *allowing* Fulr to be killed."

"Philip!" Dar gasped. "How can you dare say that? Of course, my love for the Centaurian Emperor knows no bounds!"

"Hey, watch that talk," Joe called up. "And I thought I told you two to get back to the damn Pod."

"Something is *happening* to me, Philip," Dar went on as if Joe hadn't said a thing. "It's impossible for a Martian not to tell the truth, and yet I *haven't* been telling the truth. How can that be?"

Joe got off his mattress. "Dammit, what's going on up there? You're really disturbing the Head up there, you know!"

"Naw, man, we're just talking," Sperry drawled. "Dar here--"

"We're just talking, *sir! Sir!* I won't have this disrespect on my ship!"

"Aw, forget it, Joe. Nobody appointed you captain of anything. We're all just drifting back to Earth on a wonderful twenty-one-year journey."

"Sperry, that is completely insubordinate! And possibly treasonous, I might add! Why, if the Emperor heard that--"

"Well, of *course* the Emperor heard that. But what the hell is he gonna do about it way out here? We're cruising away from him at one-fifth light!"

"You--you--"

"Listen, Dar, maybe that's why you and Kner stopped transmitting any thoughts," Sperry went on. "Maybe Fulr's death showed you guys what a pile of crap all this conversion stuff really is. Maybe you knew you'd wind up transmitting that fact to everyone, so you just stopped."

"Goddammit!" Joe shouted. "Sperry, you just stop that talk! Stop it!"

"Everything a lie?" Dar cried. "Love of the Emperor? 'Oh, Most Holy Head?' Everything, Philip? My God!"

"But that's what you're thinking, isn't it? You hate the Emperor for killing Fulr. You hate everything that's happened since we converted."

Joe's mouth hung open. Phil Sperry stood on the catwalk uttering the most obscene blasphemy possible, and somehow continued to live. And Dar nodded in agreement and also continued to live. Joe shielded his eyes from the surging radiance of Dar's mind.

"I *cannot* lie," Dar said in wonder. "In fact, I must bring up my thought radiation to full power!"

Sperry laughed. "Wow! You're back, Dar! Full strength!"

"Even if Fulr died senselessly, I must accept it, and radiate my true self!"

"*No!*" Joe screamed, rushing up the ladder past the locked Control Room hatch and charging down the catwalk. "You're traitors! Both of you! Slandering the Emperor!"

"Well, look, Dar, let's try the following concept on for size," Sperry went on. "Get this: the Emperor is an evil chopped-up piece of crap, he's disgusting to look at, the only way he can maintain his psychotic little empire is to personally brainwash every single AC that exists, and you and I are completely through with all that nonsense. What do you think of that?"

"Hmm," Dar said, nodding. "I think you may have hit the nail on the head, my friend. How could we have been so deluded, Philip?"

Sperry frowned. "Damn if I know."

"Hey!" Joe shouted, flailing his arms. "Hey! Hey! Hey!"

"So what's the problem, Mr. Hotshot?" Sperry said. "Have we left anything out?"

"You--you--treason! *Treason!* You've blasphemed the Emperor! The source of all *existence!*" Joe mustered the deadliest Stare of Head he could, a stare to channel the full force of the Emperor into instant death for the apostates. But he felt every scrap of energy flooding out of him. He hung on the catwalk railing, legs quivering. "You ... you can't contaminate *me*. I don't know how you've done it, but you've turned from the Emperor! But you won't make *me* turn away!"

"Hmm," Dar said, huge purple eyes calmly sizing Joe up.

Joe couldn't believe it. A moment ago he'd been half asleep, stoned on the Head, and now the universe was splitting into *insanity*.

"Here's another thing to consider," Dar went on. "I've just gone to full strength. Now everyone on board knows that the two of us have deconverted. The concept that the Emperor is really a hideous collection of crab guts in a box is now fully open to everyone's perusal."

"No ... please, *no* ..." Joe gasped.

Sperry peered down at the fuselage floor. "Are you and I and Joe the only ones in the *Typhoon* now?"

"I think so," Dar replied.

"Then we probably ought to seal the main hatch down there. The rest of them'll be after us for sure. Joe here won't be a problem, I don't think."

"I don't think any of them will be a problem. Surely they'll understand how joyous it is to return to sanity."

"*What?*" Joe gasped. "*What* are you saying? How can you be *saying* these things? I--I don't *like* this!"

"Just sit down and relax, Joe," Sperry suggested. "Just sit down on the catwalk and take a deep breath. Everything's gonna be all right."

Joe put his ass on the metal catwalk and gulped air. "No good! No good! It's not working!"

"Give it some time, Joseph," Dar suggested. "Let's all sit and relax."

The other two sat to either side of Joe. He could feel them working on him with awesome powers of tenderness and concern. *Unwanted* tenderness and concern. "How can you guys be giving the orders?" Joe moaned, fighting back tears. "I'm supposed to be the captain!"

"Take it easy, Joe," Sperry said, pointing to the open floor hatch to the Pod. "Well, nobody's charging us. And I'm still not getting anything out of Kner."

"Nor I," Dar replied. "Kner went a lot deeper into the depression than I did. I think he's trying to put himself into the *Kuth'rr'kq*."

"What's that?"

"The Four-Hundred-Year Martian Hibernation. Something we Martians used to do thousands of years ago before our civilization arose. We can only invoke it now in the case of life-threatening injury. I've seen Kner trying to slip into it several times over the past few weeks."

"God, sort of like the catatonia Bobby's been in."

"I'm more worried about Bobby than Kner. No one's even seen him since we came on board. He's just been locked in Pod Room Six for three weeks now."

"I know. I keep checking the medical readout for Pod Six. I'm getting readings for good physical health, so we know he's been eating, but I'm afraid he's gone. He never took conversion, but then again, he didn't stay sane, either."

"You guys ..." Joe whined. "Saying all this stuff about the Emperor, being traitors!"

By way of answer Dar patted Joe's knee. "Perhaps Kner will now respond to my thoughts. He'll be picking my vibrations of sanity. Of freedom from the Grid."

Joe shuddered. "*Freedom* ... that's not possible, is it?"

"Yes, Joe, it's possible. Phil and I just did it. Soon you will, too."

"But, Dar," Sperry said, "just look at this place! We've got twenty-one years on board this thing!"

Dar considered the closed Control Room hatch. "We were programmed not to go in there, but of course, the conversion's gone for us. Could you pick that electronic lock and pilot the *Typhoon?*"

Joe blearily followed their gazes. "Sperry ... Sperry pilot my ship?"

Sperry considered the hatch. "Huh. That's an idea. If I could hack into the ship's computers, I'm sure I could bypass it. Might take an hour or two."

"*No …*" Joe whispered. "Absolutely not!"

"But what good would it do even if I could get to the controls? Without Star Drive, all we can do is drift at one-fifth light for twenty-one years."

"Assuming the autopilot really is set for Sol," Dar said. "I've just had the worst suspicion that they could easily have fired us off in a random direction."

"Oooh, that *is* a thought. I could at least make sure the autopilot is set for Mars, and program a deceleration when the ship gets there. At least some of us might live to get home."

"I have several thousand years of life left, so the wait is of no real importance to me. But I can imagine that you or Joe might fear for your mortality here. Do you expect to die aboard the *Typhoon,* Philip?"

Sperry sighed. "Maybe, maybe not. I imagine some of the humans might."

"You're the ship's doctor. You can keep them alive."

"Not if they don't have the will to live."

"Well, in any case, perhaps you should begin to get to work on that hatch lock."

"Please, no!" Joe sobbed. "You're destroying the Head! Destroying *me!*"

"Okay," Sperry said, standing up. "There's a console right here in the Sensor Room."

A shout came from below. "You all just stop tampering with the Holy Program! We know what you're up to!" Ben McCasland climbed out of the passageway from the Pod. Behind him came Catherine Protor, then Patrick James, Will Connors, and Lee Borman. Everyone on the ship was here except for the catatonic Kner and Bobby.

"Thank God!" Joe gasped. "Thank God! Thank the Emperor!"

Sperry shrugged. "Okay, everyone, listen up. As you've probably realized from reading Dar's mind, things have changed. Dar and I have formed a sort of provisional government for this ship. We're going to be leading things from here on out."

"No!" Joe cried. At last he found the strength to stand. "Everyone! Listen to me! These two are traitors to the Emperor! I'm the ranking officer here! Sperry, either Reconvert this instant, or I'll beat the crap out of you!"

Sperry folded his arms and smirked like the blasphemous turncoat he was. "C'mon, Joe, you're on the edge of deconverting yourself. Why don't you just admit it?"

"You--you--" Damn, all Joe's energy was *gone* again. How could the Emperor let him down like this? Was Sperry right? Were they just hurtling further and further from the Emperor, leaving his Domain, losing Paradise? Dar and Sperry moved past him on the catwalk and went down the ladder to confront the Converted on the fuselage floor. Joe ran after them. "No! We're going back to Sol! To the United System! The Emperor has decreed it!"

"Joe's right," McCasland said. "And as ranking officer of the refugees, so to speak, I can say that the Emperor's next task for us is to help spread the Centaurian Revolution to Sol."

"You birdbrain," Sperry shot back. "The AC's said they were going to launch their attack in one year. We won't get there until twenty years after that. So what good are you supposed to be doing for the Emperor?"

"Well, I'm sure he has something planned for us."

"Yeah, slow death in deep space," Will Connors put in.

"*What'd* you say, boy?" McCasland demanded.

"Just that Phil's right, I guess, that this doesn't make much sense. This whole trip back to Sol is just the Emperor's way of making Jack feel worse. Keeping us alive to spite Jack. But just think. Does anyone here seriously believe that the *Typhoon* has enough oxygen, water, and food to last ten of us for twenty-one years? Even the Pod, with all its resources, only has a year's worth of supplies."

There was a numb silence.

"He's right," Sperry finally said. "I don't know why I never thought of that. We're being sent out here to die."

"Why, the Emperor wouldn't do that!" McCasland said.

"Connors, you've Deconverted! You're a traitor! Get over there with those other two traitors!" He sent Connors stumbling towards Sperry and Dar.

"See, it's wearing off!" Dar laughed. "Welcome, Will!"

"Thanks," Connors muttered. "I just realized this whole thing is nuts!"

"All right," McCasland whined, "is anyone else gonna Deconvert? Or are you all gonna fight with me for the Emperor?"

The remaining Converted shuffled around. "No! We're not gonna turn tail on the Emperor!" Joe shouted. "There's got to be an explanation for all this! Our faith is being tested, that's all."

"Yeah," Lee Borman said. "They've got a starship standing by to take the *Typhoon* in tow just as soon as we all fully become One with the Emperor."

"Yeah, we've got to be *better,*" Patrick James said. "I know I'm not as good as I *could* be."

"What's that mean, young fella?" McCasland said. "If you're not *pure,* then we don't want you on our side!" He pointed sternly to Dar, Sperry, and Connors.

James looked back and forth between McCasland and Sperry, then ran to Sperry, crying: "My God, *Jack and Amav have been tortured to death!*"

There was another long silence. "It ... it just never really sunk in," Sperry gasped. "*Amav!* Oh, God, how could it not have registered? She's dead! *Dead!*"

"Shut up!" Joe yelled. "Just shut up! There's nothing anybody can do about it! She and Jack both chose it! They could've Converted, but they were stubborn! They wouldn't listen, and no matter--no matter what we might personally feel, they had to be destroyed! They were just pieces of meat, you know! We're all just pieces of meat to the Emperor! I mean, what's the use? We're all just meat, getting further and further from the Emperor with every second!"

"God, I never considered that she'd really die!"

"Hell, Sperry, we've heard all this crap for weeks," McCasland said. "How much you had the hots for her and all. It was disgusting. I mean, if you've got the hots for someone, you just go ahead and fulfill it. Right, Catherine?" He pulled Catherine Protor to him with a lusty grin.

"Right," she said. "Phil was always uptight, even when he was Converted."

"*Dar,*" Sperry moaned. "I can't take it! Amav and Jack, *tortured!* What about that thirty-five-day torture? Then it's only been twenty-one days since it began! They might still be alive! Getting worse and worse pain!"

"Philip, we shouldn't dwell on that," Dar put in gently. "As I recall, the Maximum Torture was given no time. One can only hope they're already dead."

"God, I can't believe it!"

"Knock off the crap about the Amav bitch! We're tired of it!" McCasland rasped.

"Just shut up! I loved her, and Dar, it was crazy! I knew all along she'd never be mine! She was for Jack! And Jack was my friend! Why did I do it? Why did I waste my life like that? Why didn't I just find my own woman?"

"Philip," Dar said, "when you were in the Pod, you never opened up like this!"

"I could never be this honest before! It took being brainwashed to admit to everyone that I wanted her! But to find out the real truth--Dar, that it wasn't really love! It was just desperation! And when I finally saw her naked, when we were all captured, it was just shameful! I knew it was stupid even when I was converted! I just wanted to die at how meaningless it all was!"

"And now you see fit to entertain us all with your newfound *honesty,* do you?" McCasland sneered.

"No, the fact of the matter is that Philip Sperry has just solved a particularly vexing problem for us Martians," came a new voice. They all turned to see Kner climb out of the Pod.

"Kner! You're back!" Dar laughed. "And fully radiating!"

"Yes, just as Philip is doing at this point," Kner said. "You see, Mr. McCasland, we Martians have been exceedingly frustrated because we've never been able to read human thoughts, or rather, you humans refuse to *project* your thoughts. Now, I was lying on my bed in Pod Room Four listening to Dar's radiation of this entire conversation. What finally broke through to me was when Sperry started radiating himself."

"What?" Sperry said.

"We see now that it is possible for humans to radiate, although admittedly at a far lower power level."

"Why, yes!" Dar said. "The *K'narij* Power Flux Equation! If you rotate the axis of inversion and calculate the *area* of--"

"Exactly! The only obstacle to humans radiating their thoughts as we Martians do is that their need for privacy has always enabled them to tell lies. Phil couldn't radiate because he was being fundamentally dishonest with himself. But this has changed. Can we not all feel the sense of inner honesty now radiating from Phil here?"

"It's true, Philip, you're radiating! You've found yourself!" Dar said. "I find this delightful to bask in!"

"Y-yes, you're right! Me too! I mean--delightful!" Lee Borman wailed as he rushed to Dar. "I mean--wonderful! To bask in! God, I've been an idiot! A brainwashed idiot!"

"Jack! Amav!" Joe cried. "They're *dead!* My brother! Those monsters killed them both!" He felt his soul crack open into hysterical sobbing. He fell to the floor and felt hands lifting him up. Borman, James. *Comrades.* From far away he heard Sperry: "And now we have our crew back. I'm retaining command for a moment, until Joe recovers. Ben, Catherine, are you about to admit you've been brainwashed?"

"Not on your life, jerk!" McCasland snarled as Joe gaped at the clown he'd worshipped a few seconds ago as the Emperor's Mystical Deacon. "Cathy here and I are evidently the only people with any sense left! The rest of you are cowards! Get your hands off me, you filthy finback!" he snarled, thrusting away Kner, who was patting McCasland and Catherine as if to make them deconvert by his touch.

"You'll never radiate," Kner said, "you'll never know inner peace, until you break this brainwashing and discover your inner--"

"All right, then, have it your way!" McCasland screamed, letting fly with a fist and decking Kner in the nose. McCasland jerked Catherine toward the Pod hatch. "You can try and turn your nasty ship around and do harm to the Emperor! But he'll blast you to atoms! Catherine and I will take the Pod and drift to Sol! We'll fulfill the Emperor's commands!" They backed down the open hatch and McCasland slammed it shut behind them.

"He can't mean to jettison the Pod!" Connors said. "He can't do it from there!"

"He can! There's a backup circuit in there. I remember telling him about it right after I converted!" Sperry shouted, running for the hatch and twisting the wheel to ensure a secure seal on the *Typhoon* side. "I hope the idiot remembered to--"

A tremor ran through the *Typhoon*. "He's jettisoned!" Sperry cried. They all ran to the portholes. Joe got up and followed. For long seconds they stared in silence.

The huge saucer Pod shot away, streaming a ghostly fog.

"What--what is that cloud?" Dar said.

Joe exchanged a glance with Sperry, then took a breath. He was finally back. Able to resume command.

"That's the Pod's oxygen," Sperry said. "Ben didn't secure his own hatch. When he jettisoned, his air shot out the hatch. And it's blasting the Pod away like a rocket engine." He turned to Dar. "They're dead."

"And Bobby?" Dar cried. "Bobby was on board!"

"God, no!" Joe grunted, running down the fuselage and up to the Control Room. "The Pod staterooms do have oxygen storage tanks, but the pressure loss--God!" He pounded on the locked hatch. "We've got to try! If we can go after the Pod-- dammit! Open up! Goddammit, open the hell up!"

The hatch swung inward. Joe stared.

"There's no need to curse, Mr. Commer. All you need do is knock."

"What--in the world?" The rest crowded behind Joe.

Bobby Athens sat in the command seat. "I had it locked because I didn't want any interference as long as there was a single Converted on the ship. Now I need to concentrate on this navigational program, so if you'll excuse me ..."

"What on earth are you doing in the pilot's seat?"

"Why, learning to fly the *Typhoon,* Mr. Commer. Anyone can learn in three weeks by following instructions on the computer. We're almost ready to turn around and pick up Jack and Amav."

"Are you crazy? They're dead! Or being tortured!"

"They're very much alive and in good health. Look, gentlemen, I do need your help. We can get to Jack and Amav quickly. I know exactly where they are."

"Are you kidding? We don't have the Star Drive capability to go looking for them!"

"We now have the parts for the Star Drive. I had them smuggled on board. There was a sympathetic Centaurian named Polot. After Station One fell he was in charge of classifying all the spare parts captured there. He got the ones we needed, and he also happened to mention the location of Gnarax, the Centaurian planet for their so-called Maximum Torture."

"I can't believe this! A twelve-year-old boy flying the *Typhoon?"*

"Of course, I'll turn command over to you, Mr. Commer. That is, if you feel fully recovered."

"Y-yes, but I still can't--I mean, God, Bobby, are you some sort of Centaurian in disguise?"

Bobby shrugged. "No, Mr. Commer. What you see in front of you is a twelve-year-old human being working to the full extent of his capacities. I wonder if anyone has ever seen that before. As for the Centaurians, it's interesting what you can do by pretending to be catatonic and then tapping into the Grid. You make all sorts of amazing contacts. I even knew what the Maximum Centaurian Torture was weeks ago, before we were captured, and disguised it in a diary entry to Jack."

"I still can't believe this!"

"You should. After all, you yourself are working at the full extent of your capacity this instant. Like Phil, like the Martians, in fact, like everyone here, you are a radiator of thought. Can't you feel my radiation as well?"

Joe studied his boots.

Yes, I can feel it. I can feel all of it, from everyone. I've always felt it and just never knew what it was.

"Get going, I guess?" he muttered.

Will Connors stepped to his Navigation Room. "Thanks for the coordinates, Bobby," he called back. "Course for Gnarax laid in!"

"Where are those Star Drive parts?" Phil cried, backing down the ladder and moving to his engine.

Joe shooed Bobby into the copilot seat and punched the intercom. "Okay, all hands!" he shouted. "Man your stations! Let's go for it!"

About the Author

Michael D. Smith was raised in the Northeast and the Chicago area, then moved to Texas to attend Rice University, where he began developing as a writer and visual artist. His Jack Commer, Supreme Commander science fiction series is published by Sortmind Press. In addition, Sortmind Press has published Smith's literary novels *Sortmind, The Soul Institute, CommWealth, Akard Drearstone,* and *Jump Grenade.* All titles are available from Amazon.

Smith's web site, https://sortmind.com, contains further examples of his novels and visual art, and he muses about writing and art processes at https://blog.sortmind.com/.

Amazon author page
https://www.amazon.com/author/smithmi/

The Jack Commer, Supreme Commander Series

The Martian Marauders
Jack Commer, Supreme Commander
Nonprofit Chronowar
Collapse and Delusion
The Wounded Frontier
The SolGrid Rebellion
Balloon Ship Armageddon